The GIRL *in the* IVORY DRESS

A Ghost Story

STEVE GRIFFIN

by Steve Griffin

The Ghosts of Alice:
The Boy in the Burgundy Hood
The Girl in the Ivory Dress
Alice and the Devil

Other Supernatural Thrillers:
Black Beacon: A Christmas Ghost Story
The Man in the Woods

The Secret of the Tirthas (young adult):
The City of Light
The Book of Life
The Dreamer Falls
The Lady in the Moon Moth Mask
The Unknown Realms
Swift: The Story of a Witch (*prequel*)

The Burning Man

1.

Alice Deaton was talking to the visitors but she was looking at the ghost.

That sharpness in the girl's look, the close-set, fierce eyes, that nasty cut on her cheek… What had he done? What had that man done to her?

'…and I'll show you the key features of the Capability Brown landscape, the Grecian Temple and the boat lake,' Alice continued, running on automatic. 'And, for those of you with a taste for the macabre, we'll see the place where the terrible Lord Ashford committed some of his crimes.'

Amidst the assembled group standing in the gravelled forecourt of Farthingbridge House, a man with a ponytail and red shoes spoke up. 'Allegedly. Don't they think it was his servant now?'

There's always one, thought Alice. A memory flashed in her mind, of waiting and catching the ghost girl in the Summer House at night, of how Alice had moved into her ghostly aura and sensed – just fleetingly, before the girl vanished – the depth of her fear. Or rather, of her blind terror. Alice was certain, in that one moment, that the revisionist historians were wrong.

'Some do, but I don't,' she said.

'Oh really, how come?' said the man, adopting a teasing tone.

Alice felt like snapping at him, but instead looked back at the spectral teenager in the Victorian dress. The girl's body shimmered with the daylight, but her eyes were surprisingly dark, unnerving.

'Come on, then,' said Alice, ignoring the man and turning on her heel. 'First we go this way to the Gold Room and the Bösendorfer piano – played by no less than the fabulous old crooner himself, Bing Crosby.'

The group turned and followed her obediently back towards the front doors of the great ivy-wrapped country house.

When Alice glanced back, the girl in the ivory dress was gone.

2.

But she wasn't gone for long.

As soon as the group formed into a patient semi-circle around Alice in the Summer House down by the lake, the girl was there again. She was standing straight as a pole in between an elderly woman and a man in a gilet. She was looking hard at Alice, emanating eerie expectation. It made Alice stumble over her words.

'As you can see, not quite what you'd manage of – sorry, expect – when you hear of a Summer House,' she said. She swept her arm behind her to encourage everyone to look away from her and around at the high-ceilinged hall, furnished with a hexagonal Queen Anne table and two chairs. The chandelier on its long bronze chain looked particularly stunning, scattering stars of sunlight high over the cream walls.

'There was some suggestion that it was built as a retreat for monarchy, perhaps Queen Victoria herself, but there's little evidence of it. It's been used for all kinds of activities since, including a hunting lodge. The Trust rents it out seasonally for short stays.' She threw another glance at the ghost, saw her shifting now as if from leg to leg, in her off-white dress with its pearl beading. The girl's shoulders lifted up and down alternately. Alice could almost feel those eyes on her, emitting a pulse of anticipation. She was creeped out, knowing there was something the girl wanted, needed, from her. But what?

'I will help you,' she said, giving the girl a short, hard stare. The ghost was often in the forecourt with the visitors, but Alice had never seen her appear twice on a day like this. What did she want?

Alice looked at the surprised and expectant faces of the people around her. She considered trying to adapt her unusual statement into her narrative – *I will help you form a picture of what it was like here, the snake-thin Lord Ashford swinging his gun over his shoulder, addressing his party of shooters…* No, that wasn't going to work, just ignore it, carry on…

'This way,' she said, leaving a few baffled faces following her through to the bedroom, with its squat four-poster bed shaded by crimson curtains. She glanced back one more time, scanning the crowd – but the girl was gone again.

What did she want?

3.

'Thank you so much, that was fascinating,' said the elderly lady with the high cheekbones and long grey curls. 'I never knew about Durnsford's connection with the Maoris.'

'Yes, it was a lifelong passion for him,' said Alice, as she led the group back through the forecourt. 'He was planning to build a full *Wharenui* meeting house in the grounds when he died.'

'Really!'

Alice turned and spoke to the group. 'Thank you again for your visit to Farthingbridge House today. I hope you enjoyed it.'

There were nods and muttered thanks.

'Those of you who need to collect your bags follow me through to the main hall,' said Alice.

A small group filed in behind her, past John and Catrina, the two middle-aged volunteers in the small foyer that was filled with boots and shoes removed by the guests.

'Did she tell you all the fruity tales about Lord Ashford?' said John to an awkward-looking teenager with bunches, who turned away sharply towards her parents.

'John!' hissed Catrina, rolling her eyes in exasperation and then looking at Alice who gave her a small nod.

'This way,' said Alice loudly.

But as soon as they came through into the central hall with its dark carved wood, fireside armchairs and looming gallery, Alice could tell something was wrong.

She looked for a volunteer or member of staff but the area was clear.

'Can you smell that..?' said the lady with the long grey hair.

Alice felt a sudden twist in her gut as she realised what it was. Something was burning.

'Smells like smoke,' said a young man in a brown donkey jacket.

At that moment, the burning woman appeared, clutching hold of the gallery banister above them.

4.

Alice and the members of her group gazed up in horror as the woman – it was Femi, the room steward, Alice recognised her now – screamed and pivoted over the banister, sliding down the giant Venetian tapestry, flames trailing her fall. She struck the floor with a dull thud, at the same time as the fire alarms began their high-pitched keening.

'Quick!' said the man in the brown jacket. He ran towards the burning woman, followed by Alice and a couple of the others.

Everything sped up. Miraculously, as they drew near the woman they could hear her groaning, even as her dress and the tapestry burned. For a second, Alice took in the giant, blazing hooves of the horse of St Eustace on the tapestry, then she was kneeling down with the men, helping them pull Femi away from the fire and smother her with a rug.

'Get her outside,' the young man was shouting, and before Alice knew it three of her group had lifted the injured woman and were running her out of the Hall, which had already been vacated by the rest of the party.

John and Catrina were in the doorway, looking at her in bewilderment. Alice shook her head, stumbling back from the heat of the burning tapestry. It was incredible. Her training kicked in.

'Emergency services,' she shouted to Catrina, who nodded, her mobile already in hand.

Alice ran to them, glancing back over her shoulder.

'It's out of control,' she said to John, as Catrina began to speak loudly into her phone. 'Can you go round the side, check Liz has opened the French windows in the Gold Room. If it's safe, go in and get any visitors out!'

'The Gold Room, Liz, yes, OK,' said the man, shaking his head and running out of the building.

'You go out too, Catrina, look after Femi,' said Alice, tugging her radio out of its holster and switching it on. 'Major fire in the Hall and gallery,' she said. 'Evacuate the building. Repeat. Evacuate the building.' She thought for a moment, watching the orange tableau of the blazing tapestry, the burning rug. Then she pushed the button on her radio again and said: 'Code-19. Repeat. Code-19. Over.'

5.

It was the emergency code to save the collection. A barrage of competing thoughts was threatening to overwhelm her. She wondered if she should be out with Femi, but there were enough people out there to help her and Catrina was a good, trained first aider, no, she had to…

Alice looked again at the flames, lapping around the gallery. She glanced at the immense Frith above the hall mantelpiece, the one with the Belgian family and the girl Alice was sure was the ghost girl in her white dress – but realised there was no way she could get it down on her own. There was the cabinet, with its priceless ceramics and clocks… Was there anyone upstairs? She needed to check – but those flames…

Shaking her head in disbelief, Alice took a few steps towards the fire.

'What are you doing?'

She looked round to see Charles, the cloak room volunteer, emerging from the side corridor. He was wearing his customary yellow bow tie and navy braces.

'My God, that's spreading fast,' he said.

'Code 19, Charles,' she said. 'It's the Emergency Plan to save what we can.'

The elderly man looked aghast at the burning hall. Grey smoke was pouring over the gallery, filling up the corners, obscuring the grandfather clock and back wall, hazing the air.

'Only if it's safe, Alice,' he said. He lifted his fist to cover his mouth as he coughed.

'I… you get out,' she said. 'Take the things from that table straight out, don't worry about the protective equipment, it's too late for that. I'm going upstairs – there might still be people up there – and… the Caravaggio…'

'Alice – it isn't safe,' he said, touching her arm.

But she ignored him and bounded up the carpeted stairway towards the gallery.

When she reached the top, it was clear the gallery corridor itself was a no-go. The carpet was a sheet of flame and the pictures on the walls were burning. Fleetingly, she thought of the Ming and the French clocks in the master bedroom – gone. She couldn't risk it. She hoped that downstairs they would have time to get the Bösendorfer out of the French windows. She shuddered, thinking of how many people they would need to shift it at speed. Could they get that many people together in time?

Alice turned and looked up another small flight of steps to the Drawing room corridor, with the guest rooms beyond.

'Hello!' she yelled. 'Anyone up here?'

She jumped up the steps.

'Anyone around?' she cried again, moving down the hallway with its small portraits of ladies, peasants, po-faced children, all lit by their own little lamps. Precious – but not enough. There was a thumping and suddenly a fair-haired man and woman, visitors, were coming down fast towards her. She saw the shock on their faces as they registered the fire behind her.

'No, not that way,' she said, running forward and grabbing the man's arm. 'Turn around, back down here, there's a servants' stairs, just – there, yes, there! Is there anyone else down that corridor?'

'No,' said the woman.

'What about you?' said the man as they began to turn.

'I'm coming. I'm just checking the rooms.'

They both slowed when she said that, clearly wondering whether they ought to help.

'Just go!' said Alice. 'If you see anyone, tell them to get out. I'll be down soon.'

The woman nodded and they both turned and ran back down the small corridor. Alice heard their footsteps thudding away down the rickety staircase. She quickly checked the other rooms, just to be certain there was no one else around, then came back to the Drawing room. She flung open the double doors and took in the quiet space. Hefty curtains on two of three windows made this one of the gloomiest rooms in the house, protecting the precious contents from light damage. Alice hurried over to the far wall where the Caravaggio was hung, wondering momentarily why Femi had left the room when she was responsible for keeping an eye on the masterpiece at all times.

The painting was one of Caravaggio's earlier works of a callow boy with fruit, who critics had failed to agree whether or not was Bacchus. The few minutes Alice snatched most weeks admiring it would add up to hours of study, she adored the indolence of his eyes, the faint flush of his cheeks, the way he held his glass of wine like a Victorian lady her cup of tea, his little finger cocked. No time for looking now. She shoved aside the rope barrier and stepped up on to a low pouf to enable her to reach up and unhook the painting – and then noticed the screws, clamping it tight to the wall.

Of course! She knew it was screwed in, a basic security measure, why wasn't she thinking? How was she going to get it off? She patted her pockets for her penknife, before cursing, remembering she'd left it in the conservator's workshop.

Digging her fingers in around the frame, Alice attempted to prise the painting away. After a few seconds she realised there was no way she was going to get it to budge. She looked around the room. Could she lever it with something? No, she realised that was pointless. There would be emergency salvage equipment, including a jemmy and screwdriver, in the locked private rooms – one of which was past the master bedroom (and therefore impossible) and the other downstairs near the kitchen, which would take much too long to reach.

No, there was only one way to save it, the way they were only permitted to use *in extremis*.

She would have to cut it out of its frame.

The thought made her feel sick. The painting was worth millions. She smelled the faint acridity of the smoke and knew there was no other way.

But what could she cut it with? Policy recommended a Stanley knife, which of course she didn't have. Again, there would be one in the private area beyond the master bedroom. *Which was a great help.*

Frantically Alice scanned the tables and desk to see if there might be something she could use to cut it with, but knew there wouldn't be, the Trust would never leave anything out sharp enough to harm anyone. The letter opener? Too blunt. What could she do? The smell of smoke was permeating the room. She wanted to gag but fought it back.

She spotted a chunky crystal decanter, stood on a small drinks table with two tumblers and a Henry Winterman's cigar box. She ran over to it, snatched it up by the neck, and struck it against the mantelpiece. The decanter showered silver across the hearth, leaving her clutching a jagged neck.

Alice ran back to the painting. She had no idea whether it would work. With a shaking hand, she lifted the broken neck and touched it to the dark, upper left-hand corner of the canvas. Fighting her doubts, she forced the sharpest edge into the canvas. Once she was sure it had pierced the coarse material she drew a deep breath and sliced it downwards, pressing the shard tight against the gilded scroll of the frame.

On the second, lower edge, the crystal snapped, somehow slicing a thin layer of skin away from the top of her thumb.

'Ah!' she cried. But strangely the jab of pain she felt was in the back of her head, not her thumb. She reached a hand round to rub her neck, in the process noticing the blood dripping from her hand. What was going on? Wiping sweat from the corner of her eye, she ignored the throbbing pain in her head and the blood on her hand and resumed cutting with the other side of the decanter neck. After an inch or so it snapped again, leaving her with just the stubby, thickened opening of the decanter. She prayed that the last remaining sharp edge would complete the job.

Less than a minute later, she was gently separating the canvas of the priceless sixteenth-century painting from the backboard. The line of her cut wobbled in places, and there was one diagonal cut inwards of a couple of centimetres or so but, given the situation, she knew she had done a good job.

But how much time had she lost?

Clutching the canvas at one corner, cursing the vice-like pain in her neck, she hurried back towards the door. As she moved she glanced around, despairing at all the things she knew she wouldn't be able to save.

Even before she stepped outside the room she knew something was wrong. There was too much smoke, the air was choking, it was impossible, how could the flames have spread so quickly from the other end of the gallery?

But there it was, as soon as she came out on the landing, flames in front of her and to her left *and* right, blocking off the servants' stairs. How could that have happened? She must have taken longer than she'd thought on the painting, lost in concentration. But now the carpet had caught fire, and whilst the flames to the right were not as fierce as the gallery area, they were still too dangerous to run through. Briefly, she noticed the painting of the third Lady Ashford blistering in its frame, her pearly wig blackening.

She was trapped!

Before she could even consider making a desperate run through the flames to the wooden staircase, a surge of heat and acrid smoke made her realise it was just too treacherous. And then, just as panic set in, Alice noticed something else to her right, coming from the stairs.

Something dark and burning, moving through the middle of the flames.

6.

At first she thought it must be an illusion, just the shape of the flames, the fluctuation of darkness and shadow amidst the searing yellow. But then she recognised something more animal at play, something like… intention.

Her throat caught and she felt her hair flush with sweat. It was a man, lunging through the fire towards her. His limbs flailed about, trunk-like, scarcely bending at elbow or knee. His face was blackened, the hair all burnt away.

Alice's heart kicked. Was it a visitor?

'I'm here!' she shouted, then coughed painfully as she breathed in a lungful of the filthy smoke. The crushing pain in her head flared and black spots flashed in her eyes. 'Come on!' she yelled.

But instead the man twisted around, his back stiff, his head tilting sideways, dipping towards the ground. Fleetingly, Alice was reminded of some of those old horror films, of Frankenstein or a Mummy, an inflexible creature forever at odds with the world.

And as soon as she had that thought she realised – it was not a man at all.

It was a ghost.

7.

She had encountered enough ghosts in her life now to know one when she saw one. Even if he was burning to pieces.

It was a mixture of the strangeness of movement, the erratic, slightly delayed response – coupled of course with a fractional faintness, the few pixels short of reality. She'd read a theory that ghosts were like a recording, endlessly replaying the defining actions and emotions that had marked their lives – or deaths. And she thought there was something true about that, but there was also something more. More purpose, and more intelligence in their interaction with the living.

Alice backed up into the room as the heat of the flames pressed into her eyes and cheeks, making her wonder fleetingly if her hair might have caught fire. Taking another disbelieving look at the burning man, the agony on his roasting face, the rictus grin – she kicked the doors shut and turned around, still clutching the Caravaggio.

'Shit!' she shouted in frustration. There was no time to think about the ghost. How was she going to get out?

The windows!

She ran to the nearest of the windows and flung back the curtain. She could see the beautiful, sculpted green landscape below, running down to the blue boating lake with a pill-white temple on its shore. Looking sharply down, she saw the staff and volunteers working hard in small groups, forming chains to get the collection out through doors, French windows, and even ordinary windows. She could hear them shouting. And now, despite the wailing of the alarm, she could hear the crackle and spit of the fire.

Alice placed the painting on the floor, her hands shaking now with the awful pressure in her head. All the windows were locked so she picked up a fire extinguisher and jabbed it through one of the panes. Glass showered on to the gravel below.

'Help!' she yelled.

Within moments Mike, the Head Gardener, was below. 'Alice!' he shouted.

'I'm trapped,' she called. 'The fire's on both sides of the landing. I can't get out.'

'You can't get down the servants' stairs?'

'No.'

Two volunteers, Harry and Flo, joined him.

'We'll get a ladder,' said Harry, their oldest volunteer, who helped Mike in the garden. The two of them set off towards the Rose Garden.

'You're going to have to catch this,' Alice called to Flo. 'It's the Caravaggio!'

The woman was already looking haggard, but when she saw the painting her mouth opened in outright horror.

'I can't!' she cried.

Alice looked around. Several other staff members were approaching. 'OK – get Ben,' she said.

Within moments Ben, a large, bearded man from the shop, was standing below her. Shaking her head, Alice released the Caravaggio, her breath seizing as she watched the priceless painting flip in what felt like slow motion as it fell towards Ben's outstretched arms, it was twisting too much, an awkward angle, it wasn't going to be easy to catch –

And then, in one deft movement, Ben had dropped one arm low and caught it perpendicular to the ground.

Alice released her breath, sobbing with the stress and the pain in her head, not daring to look at the blood dripping from the top of her thumb. She turned back, thinking she would get more objects to drop to him before the ladder arrived – but gasped, to see that the doors were already burning through. In the next moment, the flaming ghost burst through the doorway.

'What do you want?' she said.

Outside, she heard Ben shout her name.

She buried her mouth and nose in the crook of her elbow to reduce the choking smoke. Eyes watering, she peered at the lumbering figure.

The first thing she noticed was that he was not changing at all, his horrible, torched skin and patches of burnt hair were not melting with the fire. His clothes were mostly singed away, but hanging from one shoulder and around his back were the remnants of a coat, which flared around the hips – a frock coat. She looked up. The burns made the face unrecognisable, nothing more than a horrific, scorched patch of leather stretched tight across a skull. His eyes were horrific black pits, a patch of ghastly white in the left one.

'Who are you?' she said, remembering her first encounter with a ghost at Bramley Manor, the ghost that had wanted her to do something.

The burning man raised a hand, red-brown fingers with patches of bone showing like a claw. Was he pointing? Pointing at her?

He waved his hand, at all times remaining in the flame.

Alice looked round at the pictures behind her, the window. Was he gesturing towards one of the paintings? Or the window? Was he suggesting she needed to get out now? Perhaps her intention to do exactly that wasn't quite so obvious to him?

She realised she was wasting time watching his awkward performance.

'Sorry,' she said, turning on her heels and quickly scanning the room. Within the next minute or so she had managed to drop a Chelsea figure and the sky-blue Sèvres basin as well as two more ornaments down to Ben, each time seeing the figures of Harry and Mike coming closer across the lawn, one at either end of the ladder.

'That's enough now, come down, Alice!' shouted the stocky man, as she disappeared once more into the room.

Again she stared at the burning man, who was still pointing at her, or at the wall – or perhaps the window behind her, through which she was about to escape. She glanced at the oak panelling, a painting of a pastoral landscape, a bronze Mercury on a side table. Did he want her to save something else? What was he gesturing about?

'I have to go,' she said. Smoke dragged across the ceiling now, swamping the rosettes and chandeliers. Alice bent double, keeping low where there was a little more air, coughing non-stop. Her throat was raw and her lungs felt as if they were being stabbed at the top. She was increasingly light-headed.

The ghost was urgent, raising his arms again. He was staring hard at her as he floundered.

For a moment she wondered whether she could attempt to do her *thing*, to step into him and see if she could catch a glimpse of his memories. Like she had before in Bramley. But then she realised that (a) she would die if she didn't get air soon and (b) she would die if she entered the flames in which he stood. She shook her head furiously.

'Whatever it is, I'm sorry,' she said. She turned and looked out of the window. And gasped, seeing that the ladder they had brought was a large stepladder. It was set up sideways against the wall, with both sets of feet in the flower beds. The top cap – which she knew you weren't supposed to stand on – was a good five or six feet below her.

'Where's the big ladder?' she shouted.

'Down the orchard!' said Mike, grasping its base.

The orchard? That was nearly half a mile away.

'You'll be all right, Alice!' shouted Mike. 'Just hold on to the window frame and lower yourself down from the ledge. You'll be all right, I'll hold her steady.'

Alice stared at the small platform at the top of the ladder. It looked far too precarious but what choice did she have? It was either that or jump.

'OK, I'm coming down!' she yelled. She sat down on the windowsill, then swung her legs out over the edge. She was terrified about how much her hands were shaking from the headache, but suddenly – perhaps it was a final surge of adrenalin – the pain lifted and she found herself once again focused and steady. Sighing with relief, she took one final look at the burning man as she grasped the window frame. He was frantic now, thrashing his arms like a dying fly.

What did he want?

Alice glanced down, saw Flo looking up at her alongside Mike, who had a fierce expression on his face as he grasped the ladder with both hands. Harry was moving to take hold of the other side of the ladder, whilst Ben had backed off a little on to the lawn, still clutching the Caravaggio. Grabbing the bottom of the window frame, Alice swung herself round to face the building and manoeuvred herself off the ledge. Her stomach clenched as she slid quickly down the wall. She gasped as her fingers and arms took the full weight of her body, dangling from the ledge. Quickly, she swung her foot out behind her. She cursed with frustration as it struck the side of the cap, hearing the men below shout as they stopped the ladder from toppling.

'We've got it, Alice!' cried Harry. 'Try again.'

Feeling a shocking pain in her locked fingers, Alice glanced down over her shoulder. She saw the platform, stable now, and swung her right foot outwards and on to it.

'God,' she muttered. She had let go of the window frame and was now holding on to the ledge, placing both feet on the ladder's cap. Once she felt enough stability, she carefully let go of the ledge too, steadying herself with her hands on the wall of the house.

'That's it, Alice, you're on now,' she heard Ben shout from below. 'You can do it.'

Taking a deep breath, she gingerly shifted her weight and edged a foot down to the top rung of the ladder. Then, still braced against the rough render of the house, she felt with her toe for the next step. Doing her best to fight the panic that was threatening to overwhelm her, she carefully bent down to grab the top platform with her hands.

As her aching fingers made contact with the cool metal, the ladder lurched suddenly, away from the house, throwing Alice off balance. She shrieked, reaching for the wall, for the ledge, for anything to steady herself and the ladder.

'Alice!' someone cried.

But it was too late. Her precarious balance was gone. Terror seized her as she pitched backwards and outwards, towards the flagstones below.

The Plea

8.

'I brought you these.'

'Thank you, Victor,' said Alice, reaching up from the hospital bed and exposing her splinted hand, with its bandaged thumb.

'Oh, sorry, maybe I ought…' said her boss, quickly shoving aside her book on the small but crowded table and placing the tall box of chocolates down. He glanced at the young woman in the bed beside Alice, sleeping beneath the long window with a drip in her hand.

'How's Femi?' said Alice, as Victor perched on the padded chair.

'Stable.' Victor pushed at his silver parting and Alice noticed some kind of shield engraved on his gold wedding ring. 'They had to induce a coma. The burns as you can imagine were very serious. And she broke a few bones in the fall. Frightful.'

Alice felt her mood – weak enough already – pivot. There was a pressure behind her eyes, but she held back the tears. 'Her mother died last week,' she said.

'Yes. So sad. Terribly sad.'

'And Ben?'

'He's fine. A few broken ribs and a fractured clavicle – but he's already back home with his wife and kids.'

Alice thought back to the moment when that awful headache had cleared, enabling her to slide down onto the top of the stepladder – only for it to then give that horrifying lurch sideways. She remembered the sickening instant of suspension as she flailed backwards… then falling… and then colliding, not with the ground, but with someone – with Ben.

'He tried to catch me,' she said.

Victor nodded.

'He saved my life.'

'Possibly.' Victor scratched his cheek. 'He might well have done. Mike is feeling it though. He was very shaken up by the incident. I think he feels responsible.'

'He couldn't help it, it wasn't his fault.'

'Yes, I know. He said one of the ladder's feet sank suddenly in the flowerbed when you put your weight on it.'

Alice remembered the fierce look of concentration on Mike's face as he gripped the ladder below. She turned and stared out of the window at the redbrick corridor across the quad. She felt a tear slide down her cheek.

'I know it's a lot for you to take in,' said Victor. 'It is for us all. But for you, especially. With what happened… with your past experiences.'

Alice looked down. 'Yes,' she said. Fleetingly, she remembered her time at Bramley, the terrible events that had led her to this life. Her understanding that it was not the ghosts who were the monsters – it was people. And that's why she'd chosen to go for this job in Farthingbridge, with its reputation for hauntings. She somehow knew that her future was entwined with the paranormal, that she and ghosts had a strange – *infinitely strange* – bond. It had been there ever since she was a little girl, when her father had come in and found her sitting on the lap of the man who was reading to her. The man who wasn't there. The man who had revisited her one night after the traumatic events of Bramley, imparting a sense of her future to her – without saying a word. She had known it, just by looking into his sad blue eyes.

'And the house, how is it?' she said, thinking how Victor only knew half of what had happened in Bramley – the human half. Which was terrible enough, but what would he think if he knew the whole story?

'The damage is extensive,' said Victor. 'Very extensive. The roof went up badly and that took them a long time to bring under control. In fact, most of it collapsed. Bringing down most of the upper floor in the west wing.' Victor took a deep breath. 'They're assessing it now, but it doesn't look good.'

'No…' Alice whispered. 'What are we going to do?'

'Well, to be honest, it's mostly out of our hands. The Senior Leadership Team have taken it over, they've appointed Charles Wolcott as Salvage Director.'

'Who's he? I've not heard of him.'

'He's good. Comes from the private sector, but he's got a background in history, and spent a few years as Deputy Director of Public Collections at RIBA.'

'Do they know what started it yet?'

'Not really. Best guess is electrics. There's a distribution board in the roof above the master bedroom. If that was faulty…'

'And how on earth did *she* catch fire? Femi?'

'I don't know.'

'We won't know, will we? Not until she comes round.'

Victor looked at her.

'No,' he said. He took a deep breath. 'But you, how about you?' he said. 'How's the hand?'

'Numb,' said Alice, holding it up in the black splint. 'But at least that's the only thing that was broken.'

Despite Ben's heroic attempt to break her fall, she has still managed to suffer a fairly severe concussion, which was why they had kept her in hospital for a few days. She wanted desperately to talk to Victor about the ghost of the burning man – but knew she couldn't. They sat in silence for a while.

'I can tell you that the Director General is very pleased with you,' said Victor at last. 'Charlie himself is rumoured to be writing letters thanking the staff and volunteers. He's a major Caravaggio fan, you know, so you're going to be first in line.'

Alice smiled. 'You wouldn't believe what was going through my mind when I cut it out the frame,' she said.

'I can only imagine,' he said. 'But you did a good job. Considering.' He chuckled. 'And to think, you're now an intimate part of its story. Every time it's shown people will be told about the brave young woman who saved it, leaving her blood stains on the bottom left-hand corner.'

Alice thought about that for a moment. Then she said: 'What do you think our roles will be now? If any…' She wondered if this would be the end of the job. Redundancy, just to rub it all in.

'I don't know,' said Victor. 'There's little for most of us to do now it's with the salvage team. They're on site with the Fire Service. I guess we'll be looking at some redeployment – hopefully.'

'Guess so,' said Alice.

'Don't worry about it,' he said. He reached and took hold of her good hand. 'We'll look after you.'

9.

Alice was released from Warwick hospital the next morning.

With her scooter still marooned at Farthingbridge, she caught the bus back to Leamington, enjoying the normality of the traffic along Emscote Road, the petrol stations, semi-detached homes, corner shops, small parks. She needed some time back in her flat just to empty her mind of the trauma. A powerful undercurrent of half-thoughts and feelings about the fire and ghosts could run on for a while on their own. Instead of paying them attention she would have pizza, wine, read, and watch mindless TV series for a few days.

She got off her bus early and went into the Asda on Rugby Road to buy herself a few essentials, plus cards for Ben and Femi.

When she got back to her flat at the top of a white Georgian terrace she brewed herself coffee then thought about putting her laptop on. She remembered with consternation the email she'd received a few weeks before. That made her decide not to boot up. Instead, she took her coffee and pastry and sat down on the leather couch to watch one of the latest American hospital dramas.

She would not think about how the fire started, or the girl in the ivory dress, or the burning man.

She would not.

10.

In the dark cavern – the underground temple – she knows there is something she needs to do, but is not sure what. She heads to the back, the statue of Mithras staring down at her with blank eyes, lit by a dozen candles. She knows they are coming for her, she must run, get out of this place, hide… She begs the statue to tell her what she must do and after a few moments his stones lips move. 'What?' he says and bursts into flames, becoming the Burning Man, stretching his arms out towards her. She dives away from his reach, runs back into the low, vaulted room. And then she hears them, the noise of boots in leaves outside, and knows she has to get away… She climbs on to the table and sees the gap in the roof above, daylight. She stretches up, grabs the earthy bricks around the gap and realises that there is someone up there, a shadow moving against the light. 'Help me!' she yells, at once realising that the others coming will hear her and then also understanding that they haven't because she is in control of this story so they won't. 'They're coming and I need your help…' The shadow moves again, a flicker across the silvery light. She feels she knows who it is, but refuses to strain for the knowledge. There is a sound above, a whispering, metallic sound, like scissors snipping. She looks back down the long temple hall and sees the door start to open, hears a dog bark. She must get out. Now. She reaches up, grabs the brick at the edge of the gap and easily hoists herself up from the table and out into the forest. She looks around, expecting to see the person who was casting the shadow, but there is no one there.

Then she feels lips against her ear and a voice whispers: 'Soon!'

Alice sat bolt upright in bed, her heart pounding. She stared blindly at the dark contours of her room, the pale chest of drawers, the chair, the curtains glowing faintly with streetlight.

Nothing. There was no one there. With the word still sounding in her ear, she remembered Bramley, the woman with the wounded hand who had appeared in her room. She realised that her stomach was rigid and forced herself to relax. To breathe.

No one. There was no one there. It was just another of her many nightmares about Bramley.

She had done well for a couple of days, getting fresh air in the nearby fields, eating good, healthy food, and sleeping like a baby. But now, as she lay back down on her pillow, her mind became wildly alive and she began to think. Who was the burning man? Was there any chance he had caused the fire? She didn't think from everything she knew so far that a ghost could do something like that. They didn't seem to have the ability to influence the real world. They could scare the wits out of people, but couldn't make objects move. Not like in the movies.

She thought back to her encounters with the sharp-faced girl in the embroidered dress at Farthingbridge. Alice had seen her in a few places, the woods, the forecourt, the butler's pantry – but the first time she had spotted her was in the Summer House. The girl had been bent over in a corner – an empty meeting point of skirting board and tile now, but who knew what had been there previously – as if fiddling with something, or perhaps crying. Alice had been unable to tell, because ghosts never made a sound. Afterwards, she had returned several times to the same place hoping to see the girl again. When she finally did, Alice had managed to physically thrust forward into her, to get inside her, occupy the girl's inner space. Like she had done with the ghost in Bramley, enabling her to sense the spirit's memories. Within the girl's aura, Alice had glimpsed a scene, an encounter in a wooded area with a wily young man who she knew from the portraits was Lord Ashford. But almost as soon as the memory started, Alice had felt a sudden, shattering fear inside the girl. It was a cliff face of sheer, existential terror, the like of which Alice had never experienced before. The girl had vanished at once, but that fear had prompted her to believe the ghost must be one of the victims of the depraved Lord, who owned the house in the mid-nineteenth century.

By most accounts, the second Lord Ashford was a devil in human form. His father was a renowned military figure, fighting in the Napoleonic wars alongside Wellington and taking a shrapnel wound that earned him a Gold Medal but left him with neuralgia and a right hand that couldn't grip. When he got home he built up a small fortune through investments in the Cornish tin industry and the East India company. He married a woman he met in Bruges, the daughter of a minor *Jonkheer* nobleman, who according to one local diarist was neither a beauty, nor loving, nor kind, leading some to postulate that she'd used nefarious, occult means to ensnare her wealthy husband.

For ensnare him she did, and building her Farthingbridge was surely the greatest of many grand gestures he performed for her. Camilla gave him only one son, the sickly Bartholomew, who suffered at least three life-threatening illnesses in his first eight years, before blooming into a healthy and manipulative teenager who quickly garnered a reputation for cruelty with the young ladies. Rumour had it that, unknown to

Lord Ashford, his wife indulged their son in his increasingly debauched lifestyle. One historian even suggested that Bartholomew had carnal knowledge of his mother.

When his father died, Bartholomew became the second Lord Ashford and inherited Farthingbridge at the age of twenty-three. There were no more checks on his abandon. The house filled with a reckless mix of fops, thieves, gamblers, libertines and worse. Bartholomew's parties became legendary. On one of the more renowned occasions, he had the Grand Terrace built up with seven hundred and thirty-two sandbags in order that it could be flooded for a Venetian party. Carpenters constructed a raised St Mark's Square, Cathedral, and Rialto bridge, so intricate and accurate that guests gasped in astonishment. Everyone wore Carnival masks and the Bösendorfer was broken when fornicators fell on it (thankfully, a piano technician brought over from Vienna was able to restore it).

In 1842, Camilla brought her young niece Eloise across from Bruges after a family tragedy. Eloise, with a precocious and lively intelligence, instantly captivated Bartholomew. Soon he was lavishing her with gifts which the young girl lapped up. Over time, Bartholomew became increasingly obsessed with the petite Eloise, calling her his *pretty little Flemish doll* and bringing her to dinner parties and dressing her up like a young lady of society, older than her fifteen years. She used to sing and recite long poems at the gatherings, many of them penned by Eloise herself. Rumours spread like wildfire about the nature of the relationship between the two, a relationship not only acknowledged but nurtured by Bartholomew's scheming mother.

Then Eloise was summoned back to Bruges by her mother and vanished enroute. A relative, an elderly statesman, arrived from Belgium to search for her and found Camilla's story of when and how she had returned to be full of holes. Suspicion arose that something was wrong. Unknown to mother and son, the statesman had his men make enquiries. A wronged servant told of hearing screams in the Summer House one night, followed by a frightful banging.

The statesman insisted on a search of the grounds and a slashed, bloodstained dress was found in the wood a few dozen metres from the Summer House. People began to suspect Bartholomew had killed the girl, but there was never any hard evidence and a trial proved inconclusive. Yes, the girl had disappeared. But no, the second Lord Ashford could not be unequivocally convicted of her murder.

After that, the wild living at Farthingbridge ceased, or at least went under the radar. Camilla died of typhus two years later and Bartholomew became something of a recluse, although he still kept a small, libertarian entourage and rumours persisted that he hounded his servant girls with unwanted attention. There were more deaths, one of Bartholomew's hangers-on fell from the roof and the body of a young kitchen maid was found in a ditch with her throat cut. Investigations were held, and with the latter Bartholomew was once again suspected, alongside his notoriously lewd and unkempt butler. But again there was not the evidence to lead to a conviction.

It was said that the bachelor was haunted by visions of Eloise for the rest of his life, which turned out to be a relatively long one. He died on his seventy-first birthday, clutching a locket with a picture of the girl to his chest.

For years, the ghost – a girl, wearing a white lace dress – continued to be seen in Farthingbridge by residents, servants, and guests. There were no known recordings of her during the mid-twentieth century but sightings began again in the early 1960s, continuing right until the present day. Alice, whose devastating experience at Bramley had taught her she could help ghosts, find a way for them to end their tortured earthly existence and *cross over*, wanted to find and help the girl. This was one of the reasons that she had taken the job at the house. She had been helped by ghosts – so now she would help ghosts as and when she found them. It just kind of… helped her to make sense of things.

But now look what had happened. How was she going to help the girl in the ivory dress when half of Farthingbridge had been destroyed by fire?

11.

For a week, these questions and more plagued her mind.

Then one morning, just after she'd got home from a run in the park, she had a call from Victor. After updating her on the salvage operation – and telling her that Femi's condition was unchanged – he told her that there were no redeployment opportunities at the moment.

'Oh,' said Alice, suspecting the worst.

'But look, don't worry about your post,' he said. 'You're signed off for… how long?'

'Six weeks,' said Alice.

'Yes – and after that, you could take some leave. That'll give me time to work with Regional to sort things out for the whole team.'

'Thank you, Victor, I appreciate it,' she said.

After the call, Alice sat down heavily on the sofa. She stared out at the crown of the horse chestnut in front of her flat, vivid and green, its clusters of leaves heaving in the summer breeze.

What was she going to do?

It had been good of the doctor, in liaison with the hospital, to sign her off, recognising the stress she'd been through. But ever since Bramley, she liked to – *needed* to – keep herself occupied. It was the only way to keep at bay a pervasive anxiety, whose tendrils stretched into all parts of her life. She knew there were a lot of people who were good and trustworthy. But she also knew – had engraved on her damaged heart – the tortuous truth that there were those who could never be trusted. Never. And how did she ever get to distinguish between the two?

Suddenly, the email she had received a few weeks before the fire popped back into her mind.

Could she…? Whyever would she? Talk about trust issues…

But then, it would give her something to do. Something that might help fulfil her bizarre, self-chosen – and in all likelihood self-damaging – sense of obligation towards the otherworld. As soon as she thought about it, she knew she would respond to it. In spite of and – secretly, possibly, if she ever dared admit it – *because* of the sender.

Her curiosity was just too great.

Peacehaven – Thursday

12.

It was a long way to Caswell Bay.

The prior November, Alice's car had failed its MOT on eight different tests ranging from excessive rust on the wheel arches to an almost-completely shot suspension. When she realised she could get to work on a scooter in less than forty minutes, she left the car with the mechanic to scrap.

So now she was on public transport, which involved taking a train to Reading, then another to Swansea, then two more buses from there to the beautiful Mumbles coastline. She certainly had time to think.

To think about what she was leaving behind – temporarily, she hoped – but also about why she was doing this. Why on earth she had decided to visit *her*. Just because she had asked for Alice's help.

Why should she?

Why should she?

As soon as she was settled on the train, heading through the mild green fields and small woods and market towns of Warwickshire, she read the email again. It had been sent to her work email, on the 15th May.

Dear Alice

I'm writing to ask for your help because I don't know who else to turn to. I'm literally at my wits' end. It's years since I've seen you and we parted on terrible terms. But I hope you can forgive me and consider my strange request.

My name is Susannah Parry – née Pugh. Yes, that *Susannah. We were friends for a while at school but then, I don't know, I was mean to you and we fell out. We fell out in the most extraordinary circumstances. You will remember that strange, awful, shocking day with Charlotte's grandmother as well as I do. It is etched forever on my mind.*

Anyway, I am a different person now. I am married to a wonderful man and have a beautiful 2-year-old son, Jacob. Five years ago we invested all our savings in a ramshackle guest house on the Gower peninsula in Wales, where my husband comes from. We did the place up and opened for business. For a while everything went fine. But then – well, then, the ghost started to appear.

Whilst I haven't seen him, I'm told he's a man in a suit with a horrible face. An electrician told us that he saw him before we opened up but we – well, to be honest, we didn't believe him. More fool us. Now we know he is real as he has started to terrify our guests. There's been several sightings, the worst involving an awful accident in which one of our regular visitors fell down some stairs after seeing him. Whilst most who see the ghost just don't return, our reputation for being haunted has been growing online and, as you can imagine, it has begun to seriously damage our business. We are plagued by cranks – you know, the nutty ghost hunters and 'psychics' – but the normal people we need to make our place work are put off by the reviews. We will have nothing if we sell up.

I have tried to get help from elsewhere. I had a local priest in. He was worse than useless. We even swallowed our pride and booked two paranormal investigators ourselves, a ghost hunting mother-and-son team, but they just drained cash and helped us with precisely nothing.

I know what happened to you at that English country house. I read about it in the papers. In an interview sometime after I was surprised to read that there was a ghost involved, and that you helped her. I found it on that paranormal website run by that Spanish guy. Do you still see ghosts? Do you know anything about them?

If you do, I'm hoping you might be able help me. I know you have no reason to. Still, I'm asking.

Yours in desperation, and total exasperation –
Susannah

Those turns of phrase, thought Alice. *Worse than useless… plagued by cranks… precisely nothing.*

Susannah might have changed, but she could hear those words coming straight from the mouth of the fourteen-year-old girl as if it were yesterday.

Alice flicked on her phone browser and looked at a few search results for *Peacehaven guest house, Gower.*

Local B&B has unwelcome guest – from the other side… Grotesque ghost terrifies guests at remote hotel… Peacehaven Guest House, Gower Peninsula – 1.5 stars, BeenThere … Couple who invested lifesavings in Gower guest house plead for "ghost hunters and cranks" to stay away…

Alice sat back and stared out of the window. It was true, what Susannah had said in her email. Susannah Pugh *had* been her best friend at school. For a few heady months one summer they had done everything together, drama, hockey, photo club, hanging out in coffee shops on the weekend. They loved the same books, music and films. But then, for no apparent reason, Susannah had turned on her. She became contemptuous and sought to undermine Alice whenever she could. When Alice turned to another girl, Charlotte Hemingway, for friendship, Susannah took it up a notch. She spread rumours about her and Charlotte, implying they were lovers. Alice tried to rise above it, refusing to deny it because she was horrified at the thought of appearing homophobic. Susannah was cunning as well as cruel.

And then *it* had happened. The event Susannah referred to in her email. The thing that occurred on that *strange, awful, shocking day*.

Alice and Charlotte had been joined by Susannah on their way home from school, coming down a scrappy railway embankment, when an old woman had appeared. At first the three girls had been dumbstruck at the sight of her, all wrinkled and bent over, wearing what looked like a nightdress in the pouring rain. And then Charlotte had recognised her. It was her grandmother.

Who was dead.

What the ghost did next changed their lives for good. She folded the petrified Susannah in her arms and, in a silvery-black trick of the light, seemed to shake her furiously for what was probably only a few seconds but felt like ages. Then she vanished.

After that, Susannah was never the same again. She fell to pieces and kept away from Alice and Charlotte. The next year she was taken out of the school by her parents, who were afraid she was having a breakdown. Alice never heard from her again.

Until now.

13.

So why had she agreed to her strange request?

Well, because of the fire at Farthingbridge, principally. That was clear. Whilst the email had played around at the edge of her thoughts, when she had received it Alice had been sure – almost sure – that she wouldn't bother replying.

But now, when there was nothing else to do, when she couldn't continue with her job, nor try and solve the mystery of the girl in the ivory dress – well, hadn't she made a pact with herself? That, being one of the few people who were able to see ghosts, she would help them – just as they had helped her? Whilst they had often surprised and shocked her, she was not scared of ghosts. From her experience, they were the good guys in the stories. So maybe there was something she could do at Peacehaven. Maybe there was a role for her to play, like her 'guardian' ghost had indicated to her in his visitation after Bramley.

Perhaps she could help this ghost – whoever it was – to resolve whatever was tormenting him, and to cross over.

To cross over to the mysterious place, perhaps nothing and nowhere, that we all go to when everything is finished.

14.

Alice was looking at the light reflected on the wet sand of Mumbles Bay when she was gripped by a sudden sense of dread.

The bus had just passed a large group of children with three grown-ups. The kids were enjoying their summer holidays, they were bouncing in the way children do, one boy's hair lifting like straw around his grinning face, perhaps they were on a trip to the playground. But then one, two, no, at least three of them were staring up at the bus, into the bus, at her, Alice, as the bus drew past. She glimpsed sudden, serious looks, accusatory expressions on small, strangely adult, faces. What were they looking at?

Then one, the smallest of the three, a boy in an orange T-shirt, lifted his arm and pointed directly at her.

Before she could even be sure of her senses, sure that they were indeed looking at her – they were gone. Leaving her with a spasm in the gut and a dull ache in her head.

What was she doing? Why was she coming here?

She hated Susannah for what she had done.

How could she be minutes away from meeting her again, that despicable girl, after all these years? What was she up to?

Sensing the start of a panic attack, she told herself that she was in control and focused back on the dark, glistening sand, spliced with silver seawater. She could turn around and leave straight away if she didn't like Susannah. She owed her nothing, absolutely zilch.

So why was she feeling like this? She began to feel queasy, the rumbling of the single decker making her travel sick. For a moment she feared that she might actually vomit, and wondered how she would manage. Was there a bin? Could she get off in time? Did she have a bag?

Trust issues. That was what this was about. Hardly surprising, after everything she'd been through. She watched the light on the sand, then looked up and spotted the boathouse and small Victorian pier on the headland. Mumbles was beautiful.

She'd been to Snowdonia and stayed in a cottage somewhere in mid-Wales with her parents when she was six or seven, but she'd never been to south Wales before. She'd seen plenty of urban sprawl on her journey today but the countryside was lovely, the green hills where the famous Valleys began, the dense woods, and of course now the serene coastline. Mumbles Bay was glorious, a great flat expanse of sand, fringed with low, distant hills, the Bristol Channel shimmering at its edge. An internet search before she began her journey promised a string of sandy coves ahead, crowned with the endless Rhossili Beach at the tip of the peninsula. Peacehaven was not so far now, but she was determined to make the trip further out to the more famous beaches. Susannah would owe her that.

She was doing well. The distraction of the scenery had cleared the strange anxiety. There was something still fluttering in her gut, but they were nearly at the Caswell Bay terminus now – the place where Susannah had agreed to pick her up.

The girl she had fallen out with so dramatically thirteen years before.

How would she be now?

The bus lurched to a halt with a hiss of brakes.

Alice waited for a few passengers to file away, an old lady with fine ginger hair, a swarthy man with an unlit cigarette pinched between thumb and forefinger, and a teenage girl with a swan tattoo on her upper arm. When they were gone, Alice hoisted her duffle bag on her shoulder and followed them out into the warm day.

Opposite the single storey terminus was the sheltered bay, with a café on the left and a concrete plateau with steps down to the sandy beach. Gulls squawked about, restlessly touching down then pushing up into flight from a squat wall. A couple stood near the bus stop, the man in his white brimmed hat glancing around in agitation, map in hand. On the beach, a mass of sunbathers laid on towels or stared out to sea, children occupying themselves with sand and spades. By the esplanade that led down to the beach, two cars had parked on double yellow lines.

Alice scanned the cars. One of them, an old silver Mercedes, was empty. The second, a blue saloon, had a man and woman inside. Was that her in the passenger seat? Alice waited for a small van to pass and then strode across the road, looking down at the couple in the car. She veered away when she noticed the confused-cum-hostile expression on the large man's face as she stared in at him and his wife.

Clearly not Susannah and her husband.

She looked towards the beach, noticing the painfully red-and-white bodies of a nearby family, mum and dad and three sons, all chattering and eating crisps underneath the hot afternoon sun.

'Alice?'

Her head shot around and she saw a tall woman in sunglasses coming towards her, holding the hand of a toddler.

She forced a smile, said quietly: 'Susannah…'

'Wow, after all these years…' With her free hand the woman – elegant, her hair cropped at shoulder length and honey-dyed – reached out and hugged Alice around the shoulders. 'I am so, so grateful you came.'

Alice nodded, pulling back. 'Yes,' she said. 'Unbelieve… It's unbelievable.' She could sense herself reddening, sweat prickling around her eyes and nose. Something tugged in her stomach.

'And who's this?' she said, distracting Susannah's gaze by looking down at the small boy.

'Umjacob,' said the boy, squinting up at her, into the sun.

'Jacob,' said his mum.

'Pleased to meet you, Mister,' said Alice.

Jacob thrust splayed fingers covered in syrupy-looking flecks up at Alice.

'Doughnut?' said Alice.

'Yes,' said Susannah. 'He had to go for a pee-pee, so we left the car for a moment on the double-yellows. Then he spotted the cake counter.'

Alice nodded.

'We'd better get a move on, normally this spot is pretty safe, but there's a warden comes round in peak season,' Susannah continued, throwing a disdainful glance at the partner of the man with the map who was now staring at her. She opened the back door and with some difficulty hoisted the stocky boy into his car seat. There was a crunching sound as he landed, sticky fingers dug into the back of Susannah's neatly coiffed hair. 'Stick your bag down there,' she said, gesturing to the space below Jacob's feet.

Alice slung her pack in around the child who, when her face was closest to his, surprised her with a winning, toothless grin. Then she hurried round to the passenger door and let herself in beside Susannah, who was already buckling up and checking her mirror. She started the car and soon they were driving away from the beach, up on to the wooded headland. Alice stared out of the window and barely managed to suppress her alarm as Susannah swiftly switched the gears beside her. She noticed her wedding ring, a simple silver band or, more likely, platinum.

'How was your journey?' asked Susannah.

'Fine.' *No one knows what lies beneath. Act confident.*

'The Gower's not the easiest place in the world to get to.'

'Start! Start!' Jacob shouted, making Alice jump.

Susannah checked in the mirror. 'Yes, darling,' she said.

'It's beautiful,' said Alice. 'I see why you came here.' *But why on earth had she?*

'Yes,' said Susannah, with a hint of iciness that made Alice uncomfortable, remembering their relationship at school. 'You haven't been down before?'

'No.'

'I'll have to take you out to some of the nice beaches and coves. Three Cliffs Bay and Oxwich.'

'I'd love that.'

'Yes,' said Susannah. She paused and then added: 'It seemed so perfect when Gareth first brought me here. Of course, if we could just replay time…'

Alice rocked her head slowly. 'What were you doing before?' She threw another glance at Susannah's angular profile, the powdered, cream-white skin, pale lipstick, fine-cut cheekbones. She could scarcely believe it. So scarcely it was untrue. How could she be so close to her again, in a car, like this? She felt trapped and had to suppress a sudden, bewildering urge to strike her. *What was up with her?*

'Nothing exciting. Running a business with a friend. A stationery company, high-end stuff, arty notepads, elegant business cards, that kind of thing. It was OK for a while. Then I met this handsome rugger-bugger of a Welshman at a friend's wedding and he swept me off my feet. A hotel manager. Before I knew it we were making plans to run our own place.'

Alice laughed, a little nervously. 'Always knew you'd have the pick of them.' Why should she be anxious for God's sake? It should be the other way round.

Susannah smirked and said: 'You flatter me. How about you?'

'No,' Alice replied. 'A short relationship last year. They never seem to stick.' It wasn't exactly what she'd meant to say, it made it sound like he hadn't stuck around when of course the problem was *her*, her blatant commitment thing – but Susannah carried on anyway:

'He's not well now, mind,' she said. 'This bloody place has brought him right down. I worry about him.'

'Oh no,' said Alice. 'Just the stress?'

'Yes. You wait.'

'Is it that bad?'

Susannah dipped her chin. 'You can feel it. It threads the place like a poison seam.'

'Have you seen him? The ghost, I mean.' It came as a relief to remember there was business to be dealt with, no matter how bizarre.

Susannah paused, then said: 'No. Neither Gareth nor me. Just the guests.'

'I read some of the reviews. That woman – the one who scalded her arm – had really got it in for you.'

'You're telling me. The irony is, she was one of our most loyal customers. Came every year.'

'Whoops!' shouted Jacob. 'Whoops Mummy!'

As Susannah scrutinised her mirror, Alice looked round into the back. 'He's dropped his cup,' she said, arching round to retrieve the plastic beaker from the floor. She passed it to the boy, who snatched it with another grin. He waved the drink at her. 'Shoo!' he said.

'You're welcome,' said Alice.

He smiled at her, then said wisely: 'Daddy's in the woods again. In the woods.'

'He's not quite making sense yet,' said Susannah.

'He's cute,' said Alice.

16.

After another ten minutes or so, they turned off the main road and headed down a country lane with steep banks of trees on either side.

'This really is lovely,' said Alice, spotting a large bird, probably a buzzard, drifting overhead.

'Yes,' said Susannah curtly.

Alice glanced again at the side of her face. At school, Susannah had been one of the most attractive girls in the year. She still had that air about her, but age had slightly elongated her features so that now she was more horsey-looking, less pretty. Alongside the blusher she wore a little eye shadow that Alice could see behind her large glasses. Susannah was now classy, but not quite so beautiful.

She wondered what Susannah was thinking about her. Dowdy, probably, with her mousy hair, faded jeans and duffle bag. And no makeup. Alice never wore makeup.

The light through the canopy flecked across the wood-panelled dashboard. With the window down, Alice breathed in the mineral sea air. The anxiety vanished as quickly as it had come and suddenly she felt good, like she was on holiday.

'Start!' said Jacob.

'He likes that word, doesn't he?'

'His vocabulary's very jumbled up at the moment. He was a late talker.'

They reached a driveway with a white sign saying *Peacehaven Guest House* in neat script, with three gold stars beneath. A separate, lower sign on two small chains declared *Vacancies.*

'So, here we are,' said Susannah, with evident reluctance. She swung the Mercedes off the road and it rumbled down the grit drive. They passed through an avenue of limes and bumped across a cattle grid, then drove slightly upwards on to a pebbled courtyard in front of the large white house. Alice thought Peacehaven was charming, probably Edwardian, with its long, central frontage and high gables at either end. A porch for the aquamarine front door was asymmetrically positioned towards the right end of the building. The windows were tall and relatively thin, painted like the door in a pale sea-blue. There was a single skylight and a further set of windows jutting out from the high pitch of the central roof.

Susannah climbed out and opened the back door to lift Jacob from his seat.

'What an elegant house. I like the room at the top.'

'Yes, it's double aspect, with a view of the sea over the back. The old Reading room. Your room, in fact.'

'Do you know when the house was built?'

'Early twentieth century,' said Susannah. 'Around 1910, we think.'

'I guess it wasn't built as a guest house?'

'No, I think it's been a private house most of its existence. It was in a state when we bought it five years ago. The previous owner was an old woman. A designer, apparently a minor celebrity at one stage. But she was suffering from dementia and was moved out by her children several years before she died. The place wasn't exactly derelict, but very dated. We knew there was going to be a lot of work, everything needed ripping out and redoing. But that was just the start of it… Stop it, Jacob!'

Jacob squawked on her shoulder, bending his knees and then kicking her repeatedly.

'Such little angels,' she said brightly, as they made their way across the courtyard to the large front door. With Jacob still on her shoulder, Susannah pushed her hip against the door, which swung inwards.

Alice followed them inside.

17

She didn't feel it.

Turning about in the broad hallway with its patterned rug and parquet flooring, admiring the yuccas in the alcove by the porch, seeing herself reflected in a gargantuan mirror above a marble mantelpiece, looking up the staircase with its framed movie stars, Alice had no sense of the *poisonous seam* to which Susannah had referred. Across from them was an open, double doorway revealing a living room with an enormous mauve settee and another neat, log-stacked fireplace. She could see an impressive painting of the sea above the mantelpiece, all white flecked spray, cerulean blues and black rocks. No, the first impression of Peacehaven for Alice was a place of air and light.

As soon as she had that thought, something dark flittered at the edge of her mind, like a black cat darting under a bed.

'Sense anything?'

She turned sharply to Susannah, who was still clutching Jacob, watching her over the little boy's shoulder. Another irrational flash of anger – but she forced a smile. 'Too early to say,' she said.

Susannah nodded. 'This way,' she said, leading her past the stairs and a corridor that ran off through the centre of the house. They came through a doorway into the kitchen, another large, bright room with a five-burner gas hob and dark granite island. Beyond that was a dining table with a suspended light globe of spun-brown glass. At the far end of the room, a collection of toys was jumbled around tall French windows, which gave out on to a decked terrace.

'Coffee?'

'Please,' said Alice, once again feeling her normal self. 'I can see why you bought this place,' she added, as Susannah tipped beans in the coffee grinder. She looked out of the window at the wide lawn beyond the decking, the rich, green wood at its edge.

Susannah made a half-audible grunt. 'It's taken…'

They were interrupted by the sound of coughing, a harsh, throaty hack, coming from the hallway. A burly man in a plaid shirt appeared in the doorway.

'Oh, Alice – this is Gareth, my husband,' said Susannah.

'Pleased to meet you,' said Alice.

'Hello,' he said.

Alice's arm twitched as the man's expression defeated her planned proffer of a hand. For a moment she regarded him, his well-groomed reddish hair and moustache, the dark brown eyes and slightly pock-marked, weather-beaten skin. He was a handsome man, in a kind of rugged way. But oh, those eyes…

And then, his lips were creased into a half-smile. 'Susannah tells me the place you worked had a big fire? Trust for England place?' he said.

Alice nodded, enjoying the rich stresses of his accent, despite the subject. 'Yes,' she said. 'It was devastating.'

'I looked it up after Susannah told me, on the internet. There was a woman. She was horribly hurt. Is she all right?'

'She's in a coma.'

Gareth shook his head. 'Terrible,' he said.

'How about you? Sounds like you were quite the hero,' said Susannah. Whilst Susannah was English, Alice noticed the Welsh turn of phrase, probably picked up from her husband.

'Well, I managed to save the prize painting,' said Alice. 'A Caravaggio.'

'Amazing,' said Gareth. 'A Caravaggio. Wonderful. How was that?'

Alice recounted the experience of the fire, ending with her escape from the Drawing room. 'But the normal ladder was too far away and they had to bring a stepladder.'

'A stepladder? Jeez,' said Gareth, fully engaged now. 'Must have been a big one. I presume they put it sideways to the building?'

'Yes,' said Alice, nodding. 'But that meant the feet were in the flowerbeds. Almost as soon as I'd lowered myself on to it, it wobbled and lunged sideways.'

'Were they holding it?' said Gareth.

'Yes,' said Alice, thinking about the strange balancing act she'd tried to do, the sudden sideways lurch of the ladder.

'Obviously not well enough,' said Susannah. 'Were you hurt?'

'No, not badly,' said Alice. 'One of our shop staff was the true hero, he managed to put himself in the way of me and a bad collision with *terra firma*. Broke his collar bone in the process.'

'But without him…' said Gareth.

'I wouldn't be enjoying a cup of coffee with you now, that's for sure,' said Alice.

'So what's happening with the house? Will they be able to repair it?' said Gareth.

'There's a lot that's lost for good, but only in one section. It'll be closed for a long time, though.'

Gareth shook his head.

'What about your job?' said Susannah.

'We'll see.'

Suddenly Gareth looked at her pointedly. 'Well, it's an awful thing you've been through, but thank God that you're here. I hear…'

'Not now, darling,' said Susannah. 'We've just grilled her about one trauma, let's give her a chance to settle in before we talk to her about ours.'

Gareth glanced at her. 'Oh yes,' he said. 'Sorry.'

'Daddy!' shouted Jacob, belatedly noticing his father's presence. He bashed down a stack of yellow bricks that he'd been carefully stacking and trundled across to Gareth.

'Careful there, young man.' Gareth lifted him up with little effort. The boy poked at his moustache, lifting the morose scowl on the man's face and bringing out a bright smile.

18.

'Is there anyone else staying at the moment?' asked Alice, as Susannah led her up the second flight of steps to the top floor.

'Just a couple of rooms,' said Susannah. 'A guy from the Valleys; and two young men from Cardiff. All walkers. They're on the first floor, so the top floor is all yours.'

'That's where the woman who wrote the review stayed, wasn't it?' said Alice. At the top of the stairs there was an open area lit by a skylight, with an armchair, coffee table and standing lamp.

'Yes. A couple of people have seen *him* up here.'

Alice nodded. Which was why they'd put her up here, of course. But she didn't mind. In fact, she was happy with that. She wanted to find this ghost as soon as possible, to find out what he wanted.

The old Reading room, Alice's bedroom, had a breath-taking view over the treetops to the gleaming sea.

'There's no ensuite, but the bathroom's across the hall,' said Susannah. 'Let me know if there's anything you want. Otherwise dinner outside at seven? I have to put Jacob to bed, and to be honest we always eat early because – well, because our lives are so bloody exhausting.'

'No problems, I'll see you then,' said Alice.

Susannah went to close the door but hesitated. They looked at each other. 'I can hardly believe it,' she said.

'That I'm here?' said Alice. 'No, nor can I.' She fought to keep her composure, to hold the woman's gaze.

'Thank you,' said Susannah, quietly. She swallowed, and closed the door as she left.

19.

For a moment, Alice stared blankly at the closed door. There was a fire notice on it, but the words were just a hash of black strikes on white. Her shoulders were knotted, as if the muscles had wrapped themselves around an iron bar. She could feel the dull throb of a headache starting.

'What are you doing here, Deaton?' she whispered. She turned and took in the room.

It was long and thin, with hand-crafted pine bookshelves at either end and a king-sized bed in the middle. The bed had a patterned crimson cover and plumped up pillows, from which you could sit up and stare right out through floor-to-ceiling windows at the sea. There was a further set of windows at the far end of the room, looking over the forecourt.

She hadn't been prepared for the feelings that seeing Susannah had aroused in her. Not at all. As the one who had been wronged, who was now being begged for help, she'd thought that – at least, after all these years – she would be in control of the situation. But it hadn't felt like that at all. Despite the damage of seeing Charlotte's gran's ghost and the difficulties of the current haunting, Susannah seemed more like her older self than ever. The older self who was strong, confident, competent. Whereas Alice felt like she was once again the shy, awkward teenager. It was like they'd been apart for a week, not thirteen years. Everything had slipped back into the way it was.

But there was one difference. Susannah was now married, a businesswoman, a mother. She had grown up, turned a corner.

Alice went over and threw open the double windows to stand with her hands on the Juliette balcony. She sucked the air down into the bottom of her lungs and felt the warm glow of the sun on her cheeks. The tension of seeing Susannah after all this time faded a little, and she found herself wondering if this place could really be haunted. It was hard to believe, it was all so charmed. A seagull swept in front of her, giving her a hunched, perfunctory glance. Another, out of sight, cawed sharply.

Alice thought about Susannah's husband, Gareth. He was a good-looking man, strong, fit and articulate, just the type she would have imagined her friend – her *ex-friend* – with. But in that first moment when their eyes met she'd spotted something in him. A blankness. A blankness concealing something she recognised, because she had known it herself.

Terror. Despair.

He was a man trying to do all he could to mask his fear. It was all the more shameful to him because he was clearly very independent. Someone physically in his prime, proud of his life. A beautiful wife, lovely son, an amazing house and business. All now replaced by a shocking fear and shame. Replaced by this.

Whatever *this* was.

Alice looked at the shimmer of the sea. She would have loved to be on holiday, just relaxing and enjoying it. She desperately needed a break after Farthingbridge. But no. She was one of those people whose life was never going to be easy. After thirteen years, she was back in the company of the woman who had betrayed her. A woman with a broken husband and business, and a spectre in her home.

How did she manage it?

What on earth could she do to help them?

Perhaps there was nothing.

But… maybe there was something that Aitor could do.

20.

Later, when she came down, the ground floor was deserted so she headed out to look around the garden.

At the back of the house was a decked area with a cluster of metal chairs and tables looking out across a patch of lawn. Beyond that, Alice discovered a footpath leading off into the woods. She followed it and soon took a right turn where the path divided. After about ten minutes she found herself at a cliff edge, looking down over a limestone escarpment to the sea, sixty or seventy feet below. The rock she cautiously peered out over jutted forwards into the water. On the left was a small, seemingly inaccessible sandy cove; she couldn't see what was to the right. She wondered if the cove might be reachable if she'd taken the left turn in the path.

The slosh of waves drifted up to her, soft and steady against the rock. She stood there, momentarily lulled by the mesmerising sound, the hazy sunshine on the gentle but restless water. Thoughts of her mum on a beach, catching at her gossamer scarf, eating ice cream and laughing, a man with a sailor's hat squatting on a stool, playing shanties on an accordion… There was a strange attraction in the height, the distance between the tip of her trainer and the sea, virtually nothing when she concentrated on the two-dimensional reality of sight, tricked into three by the crafty old brain... Her mum keeping their car, the old Beetle, running in a parking bay while she dashed into a chippie to get them dinner, clutching a pile of fifty-pence coins… Why had she had so many 50p's, she couldn't remember now? Just the sea, sparkling and calm, the glory of the view, the scale of the height revealed by the juxtaposition of her toes on the cliff with the sea and rocks directly, just a step, below…

Suddenly she was struck by the memory of her dad, of his tragic and untimely death after a fall from a cliff in Pembrokeshire. She felt giddy, crazily light-headed, and stepped back from the edge. A layer of exposed rock caught her heel and she stumbled but managed to skip to keep herself upright. When she halted her heart was thudding and she found herself thinking of that moment of panic on the bus. She sat down on the ground and took a few deep breaths to expel a sense of uncanniness creeping over her.

She looked back over her shoulder at the woods. Just dry, dappled, still – all as normal.

She stared down at the sea, watching the gentle fanning of the waves, letting the moment pass. Her father's death – like so much else – needed to stay buried in the past. She knew only too well the weight of all the baggage she carried. One day she would need to sort it all out, if time and the quicksand of the subconscious failed to do the job for her.

Alice stood up, dusted her jeans, and walked back into the reassuring tangle of the woods.

Halfway back to the house she noticed another path leading upwards into a more orderly area of planted pines. She toyed with the idea of extending her walk, it would likely reach a higher area with even better views. But it was already late and she remembered Susannah saying that she and Gareth ate early after putting Jacob to bed, exhausted from their long days that started early with the need to feed the boy and make the guests' breakfast.

21

Gareth uncorked another bottle of red wine, glugged half its contents into two glasses and handed one to Alice. Everything – the drink, candles, a crash-prone moth, the warm night air on the terrace – was going to her head. But still, when he handed her the re-filled glass she took down a good slug.

She was on holiday after all. Or at least had no responsibilities, obligations. Beyond ghost hunting.

'I met his wife next morning in the hotel gym,' Gareth continued. 'She was –' he paused, then said with emphasis, '– unbelievably gorgeous…'

'Not quite in my league, of course,' said Susannah. She was drinking too, from a bottle of white, but more moderately than Alice and her husband.

'No darling, no one could be,' said Gareth, smiling. 'And she was very charming with it too. So you can imagine how I felt when the next day she left and the same night these two young girls turn up at the front desk, declaring they're his *nieces* and want to see him in his room!'

'No way!' said Alice, snorting a laugh. 'I'm never listening to his stuff again. What a creep!'

'That's what they all called them,' said Gareth. 'Their *nieces.*'

'All those pervy rock stars,' said Susannah.

'Fame gone to their heads,' said Alice, sipping more wine. She was going to feel it in the morning, it was already late and this was their third bottle. But Gareth's stories of his life in the hotel business were great and it was a pleasure to see him relaxed and unguarded.

Undoubtedly, one of the key skills for a hotel manager was being an excellent raconteur, keeping the guests, high and low, charmed.

And of course they hadn't got around to the big story, the elephant in the room, yet.

'I always think it must be a bit like being the captain of a ship, being a hotel manager,' she said. 'All those –'

A bang from inside the house made all three look round.

Susannah pressed her ear to Jacob's monitor, but all they could hear was the faintest, steadiest breathing.

'Probably one of the guests,' said Gareth. Alice noticed the change in atmosphere, how glum he suddenly looked.

'Do you want to talk about it now?' said Susannah, sitting upright.

'Guess we have to,' said Gareth.

He began to cough. Given that he hadn't smoked or coughed all night, Alice wondered if it might be nerves as opposed to a virus.

'I'm all ears,' she said when he finally stopped.

22.

'Owning our own guest house or boutique hotel was the dream that brought us together,' began Gareth. 'I'd been working overseas for a major hotel chain and came back to a job in Cardiff, but was feeling pretty jaded with the infighting for positions, the industry squeezes. Soon after Susannah and I married, we jacked in our respective careers and bought this place, nearly five years ago now.'

'I sold my flat and Susannah had some capital from her stationery and other business ventures. The property needed a lot of work, but for us that was all part of it. We wanted to make the place our own. We hired a few local traders, but set about doing as much of the work as we could ourselves.'

He paused and looked across the table at his wife, who was pulling at a few strands of her hair.

'It wasn't long before things started happening that were – not right.'

'You expect setbacks in every project,' said Susannah. 'But not as many as we had. The biggest cost was an undiscovered subsidence issue, which required underpinning the whole west wing of the building.'

'Bastard expensive,' said Gareth. He raised his hand to block the chaotic moth as it swung a new trajectory towards the candlelight.

'With big insurance implications,' added Susannah.

'Then there was the paint that was badly mixed,' said Gareth.

'Cornsilk Soft,' said Susannah. 'Eighty-eight litres of the bloody stuff. We only found out about the mixing problem after doing the second downstairs coat. The patches we thought would go still showed through.'

'Looked like mould,' muttered Gareth.

'We had weeks and weeks of arguments with the supplier over it.'

'A month of hard work totally wasted,' added Gareth.

'There were other things, expected things, like problems with the wiring and a faulty boiler that needed replacing. But then there was the incident with Chainey.'

'Good man,' said Gareth, 'one of my old school mates. Brilliant carpenter. He came down from Swansea to do some wardrobes and shelving and found a lot of woodworm, particularly in the skirting boards. Spent hours working late into the night after treating it, trying to keep to schedule. Then one of those nights – it was an October night, cold, raining – we were down in the kitchen when we heard him scream. Literally scream.'

'Like in a horror film,' said Susannah.

'He was upstairs, working on the Reader's room – what's now your room,' said Susannah, and Alice was sure she flushed, although it was hard to tell in the candlelight. 'We ran upstairs and met him coming down, on the first-floor landing.'

Gareth laughed bitterly. 'I told him he looked like he'd seen a ghost.'

'Which of course he had,' said Susannah.

'He said he'd been drilling at the back of one of the alcoves, working by his lamp as the wiring was still being replaced and the electric was off. When he turned to pick up a screw –'

There was a candle between Gareth and Alice and in its flapping light she saw his Adam's apple bob repeatedly as he tried to find words – or breath. He was staring at the table, at the smeared dishes of finished Eton Mess.

'Are you…?' Alice began, before Susannah said:

'The ghost was there, sitting behind him on the floor. He described it to us. A man, in a suit, with a horrible face. Frog eyes, blue lips, tongue halfway out his mouth. The ghost was reaching for him, for his shoulder. But Chainey didn't hang around, he screamed and ran away.'

'Course, we tried to make a joke of it,' said Gareth, recovered. 'Chainey of Llandaff Club seeing a ghost?

Been on the Brains again, he has. But it was obvious he wasn't even near the right mood.'

'Gareth had to take him home,' said Susannah. 'He wouldn't stay here, and he couldn't drive himself. He kept on saying how real it was, there was no way it was an illusion, how he'd seen it with his eyes, crystal clear in front of him.'

'Shaking, he was,' said Gareth. 'I saw someone with hypothermia once, this old woman who used to swim almost year-round in the sea at Caswell Bay. One year, March time, it was just too cold. I was walking my dog on the beach when I saw her come out, try to dry herself. She kept dropping the towel. When I went over to check on her, I could see she wasn't well. All white, as you'd expect, but her body was kind of shuddering, like it was being shook by an idling motor. She couldn't speak in proper sentences, said something about her child coming to collect her. I looked around the deserted beach but there was no one around. That's when I realised she needed help.

'Chainey was just like that. He couldn't string five words together.'

'Poor guy,' said Alice. 'Did you stay here on your own then, Susannah?'

'I did.' Susannah paused, her jaw gyrating slightly as she bit the inside of her cheek. 'Yes.'

'I wanted you to come with us,' said Gareth.

'There were only two seats in the van, Chainey would have had to cram in the back area. And I didn't want to spend two hours in a van when I was already exhausted.'

'Did you see the ghost?' said Alice.

'No,' said Susannah, gazing down at the tiny flames reflected in the globe of her glass. 'But I did go and look.

I was scared, as you can imagine…' she trailed off, glancing cautiously at Alice. 'But I went to look.'

And Alice *could* imagine how scared Susannah would have been. She remembered again the bizarre incident when her friend Charlotte's grandmother – her *dead* grandmother – had literally shaken the wits out of Susannah. Whilst it had at first seemed unfathomable, it had dawned on Alice and Charlotte afterwards that her gran had returned to exact punishment on Susannah for her treatment of her friends. The girl fell to pieces and, within six months, had been taken out of the school by her parents.

Remembering the incident now, she wondered briefly if that was the reason she was actually here – guilt. Despite Susannah's lies and malevolence, surely nothing could have justified such an excessive meting out of justice from the afterlife – with such lifelong implications? But at the same time, neither she nor Charlotte had asked for any assistance. They hadn't summoned the ghost, it wasn't their fault. So why should either of them feel guilty?

But still, *being her*, Alice did. Alongside this residual anger that still bubbled away. Why had Susannah turned on her after months of perfect friendship, for no apparent reason?

'It must have been terrifying,' said Alice, giving Susannah a careful look. Had she told Gareth about the incident at school? she wondered.

'I'm tougher now,' said Susannah. She looked at Alice, stared her in the eyes for a moment. Alice felt her heart kick.

'I never believed in ghosts,' said Gareth. 'As far as I was concerned, all that paranormal stuff was a load of old codswallop. But the way Chainey talked to me afterwards, all the way back to Swansea – it unsettled me. He really was scared. A thirty-five-year-old man. He kept describing the ghost, apparition, over and over again, repeating himself a lot, but every so often adding another small detail – about a mark on his cheek like stretched dough, a stain on his otherwise neat collar, his blond hair being wispy at the temples, thinning on top. It was as if he needed to convince me that what he saw really was real.

'I'd always thought he had a bit of obsessive compulsive disorder – undiagnosed, of course – and all I can remember thinking is that this confirmed it, once and for all. There was no doubt he believed he'd seen that ghost. I was hoping it was all an elaborate windup – he had a good sense of humour, Chainey, though didn't go in for this kind of joke. But I soon realised he wasn't joking. Me old drinking mate Chainey, well – he really did believe he'd seen that ghost.'

23.

'What happened next?' asked Alice, watching the kamikaze moth come up over Susannah's head and disappear into the dark.

'Nothing – for a while, at any rate,' said Gareth.

'Thankfully,' said Susannah.

'But Chainey would not come back,' said Gareth. 'He told us we should get out of the place. I said, what, with all the money we've had to borrow to pay for the underpinning? In the end I had to hire some other chippy, but he made a decent enough job of finishing Chainey's work.

'Six months behind schedule, the house was ready to open. Not complete by any means, a place like this never is, but six of the seven guest rooms were done, as well as the public rooms downstairs. We opened up that June.' Gareth paused to swig his wine.

'Things went well for a while,' he said. 'We were nervous about booking the Reading room – despite it being the best room in the house – but in the end we went ahead and did it. And no one complained, in fact, everyone seemed to love their time here.'

He lifted his hand to cover his mouth as he coughed. Then he continued: 'We almost forgot about Chainey's experience. Almost. I was hoping it was all just a vivid hallucination. The result of too much booze as a young man, or perhaps something to do with the OCD.'

'Then Mark came with his nephew,' said Susannah, rolling her eyes at the night-time sky. It caused Alice to glance up too, noticing the fabulous spread of stars.

'Mark was a crane driver from Merthyr,' said Gareth. 'His brother, from Llwydcoed in the Cynon Valley, was having a terrible time of it. His wife had died of bone cancer and he was having to work and bring up his twelve-year-old son, who was quite a handful. And coping with all that grief. Mark tried to help, give him a break, by taking the boy on day trips and short breaks. He brought him here, and we put them in the Reader's room.

'The first night was fine. They spent the next day driving round visiting the beaches. The boy, John, he liked body boarding, so Mark would watch him from the shore, smoking his roll-ups. But the next night, we all woke around two to the sound of – well, to hysterical shrieking coming from the top floor.

'I ran up, while Susannah went to Jacob. There were a few guests in that night, I passed Mr and Mrs Moore both in dressing gowns outside their room on the first floor, and then found Brian Hod, the teacher from Barry, in his tee and shorts on the second, listening anxiously outside the Reading room door where someone was still screeching. I was sure it was the boy, as I reached Brian.'

Once more, Gareth broke into a fit of coughing, and there was something horribly raw about it, like the harsh revving of a souped-up car. Alice reached out to pat his back, but he held up a hand to stop her. He cleared his throat and resumed:

'I knocked on the door, asked if they were all right. Mark opened up a moment later, saying that he thought the boy had had a nightmare, apologising that he couldn't get him to stop. Which, as soon as he said it, the boy did.

'I went in with Brian. John was sitting up in bed, his arms wrapped tight round his legs. He wouldn't look at us for ages. Mark tried holding his shoulders to get him to look up but the boy kept shaking his head between his knees and saying no. Over and over again.

'Brian at the door was asking whether he should call an ambulance? Mark said no, let's see if we could deal with it, the boy had been through a lot with losing his mother and let's give him a few minutes to calm down. He tried to put his arm round him again but John just shook him off, quite violently.

'I suggested Brian went back to bed, which he did, with some relief. Then I went down to check on Mr and Mrs Moore, and apologised to them for the disturbance. I told them John had had a nightmare. Then I made hot chocolate and tea for Mark. When I got back up, I was surprised by the stare they both gave me when I came in.

'We're going to have to leave, Mark said to me. What? I said. He said John was really scared, he saw a man standing in the corner in the half-light by the curtains. Said he had googly eyes. He was too scared to stay the night here.

'I shook my head. It's just a nightmare, I said, but no, even though Mark clearly thought the same, when the boy got worked up like this there was no way of changing his mind. He wasn't staying here tonight.

'I apologised, I don't know why, probably shouldn't have done, and Mark said there was no need. So they packed their things and left, there and then, in the middle of the night.'

Gareth drew in a deep breath, then sighed. Alice could see the lines on his face, the effort it was taking for him to recount all this. Susannah saw it too, and took over:

'Of course, the other guests were all talking about it the next morning. Mrs Moore in particular was very shaken up by it all. Mr Moore, apologetically, told me that whilst they'd visit Rhossili that day and stay another night, they'd like to cut out their final night because of her age and nerves. I told them that would be fine, of course we understood. It had been a shock for us all.

'That was the first of the guest incidents. Over the next six months there were two more – an elderly man who saw it…'

'And he wasn't even in the Reading room, he saw him by the kitchen,' said Gareth.

'And then a young woman on her own, she was in the Reading room,' continued Susannah. 'She was actually quite calm about it, didn't tell us until the next morning. She said she had seen a ghost before.'

'But then she went and left that terrible review on *BeenThere*,' said Gareth. '*This place might be attractive but don't be deceived. It's haunted by a foul spirit and has a terrible atmosphere.*' That's what she said, then described the ghost.'

'Yes,' said Susannah sharply. 'Two-faced cow. And then there was Molly, one of our regulars who used to stay with us every summer for a few days. She was going up the stairs with a hot drink when she saw him. He gave her such a fright she fell backwards, breaking her arm and scalding herself from the drink.'

Susannah leaned forward and pressed her temples before continuing.

'She deleted all her old reviews and replaced them with one which said…' Suddenly Susannah laughed. 'Oh God,' she said, 'you just couldn't make it up. Her title said it all, it was in blocks, DO NOT STAY HERE – HAUNTED BY EVIL SPIRITS. I sent her an email pleading for her to take it down but she didn't reply. We then tried going direct to *BeenThere* but they wouldn't take it down either, said that whilst it was unusual it didn't contravene their guidelines.'

'And after that, they all came,' said Gareth.

'Yes, the psychics and ghost hunters and weirdos and just ordinary folk who wanted to find out if it was true,' said Susannah. 'For a while it was actually good for business, we even thought about playing it up a bit in the press. But then we realised that the new people who were coming – well, they weren't really the kind we wanted staying here.'

'It was like scratching an itch,' said Gareth. 'Great for a bit, but it only led to more damage. After a few months the cranks dried up, all bar one or two. And then very few people came. All the regulars, those who wanted a restful break or to explore the peninsula, had been put off by the horror story reviews and the bloody freaks who were staying here.'

'Our finances began to walk a tightrope,' said Susannah.

'And you say you never saw him – the ghost?' said Alice.

Susannah and Gareth exchanged a glance.

'No,' said Susannah. 'In some ways I wish we had. At least one of us. So we could be certain.'

'Yes,' said Gareth morosely. 'But he seems intent on only scaring the wits out of our guests. Leaves us alone, he does.'

There was a moment's silence. Alice looked into the candle, feeling the weight of the atmosphere and trying to find the right words to say. Just as she was about to comment on how wretched she felt for them, Susannah said:

'Look, it's late, I think we should leave things there for now. Let's get some sleep and we can discuss it tomorrow.'

'Yes, good idea,' said Alice, glancing at her watch. It was twenty past midnight.

Without saying anything, Gareth stood up and suddenly gasped, clutching his back. Alice was surprised to see Susannah take his arm and lead him like a geriatric back towards the house.

Alice picked up the bowls and followed the couple into the kitchen. Susannah glanced over her shoulder and said:

'Gareth has a weak back. Years of playing in scrums. I'll just take him up to bed. Hang on a couple of minutes and I'll be back.'

Alice was about to say goodnight but Gareth seemed too morose as his wife led him out. It was as if he had expended every ounce of energy – and hope – in the story. She felt intimidated by his crushed look, and let them go.

She busied herself tidying up, her mind buzzing. Who was this ghost? Why was he scaring all the guests – but not Susannah, who Alice knew was one of the people who could see ghosts? What did he want, if anything? All the ghosts Alice had encountered so far had either been poor, lost souls, in need of help – or those who had in some way wanted to help the living.

Was it possible that, for the first time, here was one that was genuinely malevolent?

'I hope you don't mind,' said Susannah, breaking her reverie as she stacked the dishwasher. 'I have to take him to bed when he gets like that. It's – it's been a lot for him to handle. He was a very active man, used to run 10k every day along the coast, but now he gets so down. And that old back injury from rugby plays up whenever he's stressed.'

'Is it the ghost or the money that's worrying him most?'

'Both. But to be honest, it's the money mainly. He's not that scared of the ghost, especially as he's never seen him. It's just the fact that… well, that the bloody thing is ruining our lives. Slowly but surely. It's like gradually being throttled.'

'I don't know what to say,' said Alice. 'It's such a nightmare.'

'Yes, it is,' said Susannah. 'Look – you leave that now, I'll finish up.'

'Don't worry.'

'I insist. You go to bed. You've realised – obviously – why we've put you in the Reading room.'

Alice nodded.

'I hope you don't mind. But – you see them. Like me. Although I haven't seen *him*,' she added quickly.

'Yes. And, if I do, what do you want me to do?'

'I don't know,' said Susannah. 'Anything – anything you can, to get rid of him.'

Alice placed a last bowl in the dishwasher and stood up. She turned to face the tall woman.

'I will help you, Susannah,' she said. 'I'll help you and your husband and your lovely little boy, if I can.' She saw the look of relief on the blonde woman's face. 'But…'

'But what?'

'I need you to tell me why you did what you did at school.'

Susannah's eyes widened.

'Why you were my friend for most the year, then you tried – with some success, I have to say – to ruin my life,' Alice continued. 'I need you to tell me. Not now, it's too late and I'm too tired, as well as a little drunk. But tomorrow, when we're fresh. You tell me, or I'll walk away from you and your family. Tomorrow, with no discussion.'

Susannah stared at her for a moment, then looked away.

24

Despite the time, Alice needed to wind down after hearing their story – and particularly after facing up to Susannah, for the first time in thirteen years. No, let's face it – for the first time *ever*. At school, she had never taken her to task over what she did. Susannah would have got away with it scot-free, if it wasn't for the ghost. Who knows how much she would have made her – and Charlotte's – lives a misery, if it wasn't for Charlotte's gran?

So when she got up to the top floor, she went into the bathroom across from the Reading room and set the bath taps running. She headed back to her room to undress and put on a towel robe. Her neck and shoulders were sore and she realised she'd been tense, tense as a bowstring, as her mum used to say, listening to Gareth telling their sorry tale. In fact, she'd been *tense as a bowstring* ever since she'd arrived in Caswell Bay and met Susannah.

What a day. She popped a couple of painkillers and walked over to one of the bookshelves. They were filled mostly with thrillers and chick lit, but there was a good number of literary books as well as a few left over from the classics degree that Susannah had mentioned during the evening. Alice and Susannah had been the only two girls in the whole of their school with an interest in the classics, particularly Ancient Greece. She saw Annas's Ancient Philosophy introduction – a mainstay of first year students – and Wallace-Hadrill's *Augustan Rome.*

The lowest shelf was the height of Alice's waist, where she saw the full *Decline and Fall of the Roman Empire.* The bookshelf had been built out – no doubt by the beleaguered carpenter, Chainey – to house a set of drawers at the bottom. On the top ledge of the drawers was some cut material as well as a large pair of sewing scissors, proper dressmaker's shears, and a thimble and some pins in a pot. The fact they had not been put away somewhere made Alice wonder how long it had been since Susannah and Gareth had let out the room.

Drawing out a book entitled *Greek History*, she headed back to the bathroom.

She lay in the luxurious, roll-top bath, the eave window open to the night air, and soaked. She tried to read the book for a while but found it hard to concentrate. All around her, the building, the wood, was quiet, but when she listened hard she could hear the sea. The gentle sea, murmuring in the night.

When she got out, warm and relaxed, and headed back in the robe into her room she wondered:

Would she wake with a start in the night, staring up at a ghoulish face?

Friday

25.

First there is just a feeling, a blind, abject terror, a heart beating thick and fast as it falls through the never-ending dark, the light vanishing to a point above…

And then there is more light, detail, a large, well-appointed room – and outside, a broad swathe of grass leading down to a lake, brightness, and she is glancing around with eyes wide, breath quick in her chest, spinning around and seeing him standing in the doorway, by the bust of Berlioz on the mantelpiece, his tousled red locks and hooded eyes, the childlike face, a stirring of something exciting, a dashing hope and then he moves towards her and…

Snip, snip, snip, the terror cuts her heart and she plummets once more…

Alice woke with a gasp, the metallic taste of terror still in her mouth. The girl in the ivory dress. She felt it again, the shock of that moment in the Summer House, alone at night when she had stepped into the girl's shimmering aura…

The man with the red hair, Ashford – what did he do to her?

Alice looked around at her room, the light streaming in through the lily curtains, the rows of books, the plush red armchair near the wardrobe. As her heartrate slowed, she let the image of the man and the feeling of terror drain away.

Too much drink. That was why her sleep was so disturbed, surely. But at least she hadn't been visited by the ghost of Peacehaven. *Only by a dream of the ghost of Farthingbridge – and her tormentor.* She knew she had to solve that mystery – but only when she could, only later, when the house had reopened.

But now, since she was awake early – she had had far too little sleep – she might as well take a walk before breakfast.

As she came downstairs she heard Susannah in the kitchen, already preparing the guests' breakfast. Jacob was making garbled noises and banging something in the kitchen too. Alice popped her head around the door.

'Morning,' she said.

Susannah stopped chopping tomatoes on the island. 'Hi,' she said, then quickly added: 'Well?'

Alice shook her head. 'Nothing,' she said.

Susannah looked disappointed. 'Shame you can't book appointments with the afterlife.'

Alice smiled. 'I'm just off for a walk. A little too much wine last night. Need to clear my head.'

Once outside, she headed straight off into the woods. She turned right at the fork and then soon after followed the upward path she'd spotted the day before, through to a brighter area of Norwegian and Scots pine. After walking gently uphill for a few hundred metres she came to a darker section with a thick understorey of laurel scrub. She spotted a neat but weathered section of stone walling, presumably the boundary of some long-gone property. There was a light wind and she savoured the fresh, piney scent.

Despite the lack of any spectral appearance, she had tossed and turned a lot in the night and her shoulders were still stiff and achy. As she walked, she worked through Gareth and Susannah's story. What a burden for them to carry, the picking apart of their dreams. But what could she do to help them? She was no detective. Back in Bramley, she had managed to uncover a little of the ghost's story, but nowhere near enough to change things. The only advantage she had was her peculiar ability to *feel* a ghost's memories – but only if she was able to stand within its aura.

No, she was glad she had put her friend, Aitor Elizondo, on standby to come down – if, and only if, Susannah came clean about her motives for betraying her all those years ago.

Aitor was one of the few paranormal 'investigators' who Alice trusted. For a long time after Bramley, she'd kept the medieval manor's tortuous memories to herself. But it had been hard. Very hard. At one stage the pain had got so much that she'd thought she would have to throw in her job and check herself into a clinic. She liked to think it was something special about her, something steely inside, that had helped her cope with all that had happened. But when she did *like to think* that, she was quick to chastise herself. It was luck, first and foremost. Others far stronger than her had been through similar ordeals and snapped. No, somehow, she, little old Alice Deaton, had not been special, she had just been supremely lucky. To have an above-average resilience – but principally, to have a little help from *the other side*. She was surviving now, not quite happy, but most days calm enough. But she knew if she got big-headed about it, something twisted inside would soon gnaw away at her confidence. Something which could even bring her down, lay her low, with one swift swipe of the scythe. Take her back to that scared and panicky teenager, her fragile ego undone in a moment.

Then one day she was half-listening to a magazine programme on the radio, chopping leftover chicken for a lunchtime sandwich, when she'd heard a man with a gentle Spanish accent being interviewed about a ghost that had been seen in a Bengali restaurant in High Wycombe. The interviewer was clearly angling for a joke or two, but the Spaniard – or rather, Basque, as he'd clarified – kept repeatedly and courteously returning to the plausibility of the witnesses, as well as the history of sightings in the restaurant.

It had been enough for her to look Mr Elizondo up on the net. She found that he kept an impressively rigorous blog on the paranormal – alongside a day job as a machinist in an engineering research facility. She dithered about clicking send on her message on his contact form, before eventually stabbing the button and walking away. He got back to her almost immediately, keen on finding out more about her story. They arranged to meet for a coffee. He was a short, swarthy man, with an ear stud and thick, white-blond hair with dark roots. At once they fell into an easy conversation and the coffee stretched into lunch as Alice began to open up to him about her experience with Mary and Petey Stevens. She had never revealed the supernatural elements of the story before to anyone. She knew that any talk of spirits would have instantly undermined her credibility with the authorities.

But Aitor had understood. He had published an article about it on his website, entitled *Redressing the*

Balance – An Extraordinary Tale of Why Ghosts Remain. She thought the title a little overblown, in the gothic melodrama vein, but the article itself was intelligently written and insightful. She had let him mention her by name, but she had asked him to anonymise most of the details and other people, as the last thing she wanted was any more publicity. But also, at the back of her mind, was the thought that by putting out something like this she might, via Aitor, be contacted by someone else who had experienced something similar. After all, part of the story or meaning that she'd internalised after her experience at Bramley was that she would help the spirit world as it had helped her. Which was also why she had taken the job at Farthingbridge, knowing that there were creditable, detailed accounts of hauntings in the building through the centuries.

And, of course, it had worked. It was Aitor's article that Susannah had found, and which had enabled her to contact Alice again after all these years. After reading the article Susannah had searched for Alice and managed to find her Trust for England email address.

Alice hadn't told Susannah that she'd invited Aitor yet. He had made his booking independently and would – subject to Alice's confirmation – be down sometime the next day. If Susannah was honest with her, she would tell her then who their booked guest was.

Now, as she followed the upward path, she realised how much she was looking forward to seeing the Basque. Her spirits were leaden and she could do with a shot of his energy and optimism.

The path came out along the cliff edge, fading to little more than a loose trail of earth on bedrock. Alice stepped up on to the thin grass verge, worried that if she slipped on the gritty soil she might be propelled dangerously close to the edge. She remembered the odd, almost dreamy sensation she'd had the day before, standing looking over the cliff edge, thinking about her dad. She didn't want to experience that again.

At the top, the path levelled out and she found a hexagonal shelter, open on all sides, with a hipped roof and a 360-degree seat around its central pillar. Alice sat down, facing out across the Bristol Channel. She watched the bright water, greenish today, dabbed with spots of silver. In the distance she spotted the faint outline of land – England, Somerset or perhaps Devon, she guessed. It was a beautiful spot. A brown bird with a white underside flicked across her field of vision and headed up to the treetops, a flycatcher. She heard an engine start in the distance, something raw, untuned.

She was just about to stand and resume her walk when she had the sudden, uncanny feeling that she was being watched. It came as a physical sensation on the back of her shoulders, as if they were being brushed by something, perhaps a feathery branch. She spun around, looking to the side of the shelter's central pillar, back into the pine forest. Still, tall trees, stately, dramatic. Peaceful. Like a theatre, or temple. All quiet.

There was no one there. Quickly, she stood and paced around the structure, looking in all directions, back down the crumbly path, out to sea, through the trees. She glimpsed a sudden motion out of the corner of her eye, off slightly to the left, but as soon as she twisted around realised it was just another small bird, skimming from one tree to the next.

There was nothing else there. *No one else there.*

But she'd felt it, felt sure there was someone behind her. Right behind her, almost touching her. She remembered one of her history lessons at school, when their elderly teacher Mr Abraham had told them about Ptolemy's emission theory of optics. In that, the eyes were supposed to work by sending *out* rays of light to see objects. She thought now that the theory seemed apt. It was as if her back had been touched, ever so faintly, by beams from someone else's eyes. Someone now hidden in the forest.

'Hello?' she said. Her voice sounded flat. 'Hello,' she said again. She listened hard, to the faint swish of the sea. And then she heard another noise, a crisp, scissoring sound. Closer, more definite. She jerked around but again the forest was silent.

Perhaps it was the hangover giving her dark imagination greater reign? She rubbed her neck, pushed her thumbs against the muscles. They were rock hard. They got like that when she was doing a lot of typing under deadline at work. But this time, she was sure it was just caused by the disturbed sleep of the half-drunk. She had to admit, she didn't feel that great. She would lay off the booze tonight.

Feeling increasingly on edge, she made a final, careful scan of the woods, sea and shelter. Still seeing nothing untoward, she decided to carry on. The route continued for a few hundred metres and then began to curve back the way she had come. She followed it – once again hearing that unpleasant motor in the distance – and soon came across another section of standalone wall on a small, laurel-wrapped mound. Intrigued, Alice worked her way around the edge of the foliage and discovered an old brick foundation in the ground. The wood had largely reclaimed it, over-layering it with a mixture of laurel, snaky young trees and stretches of bracken. She followed the foundations through the woods, becoming increasingly convinced that this was not a private house as she had at first suspected.

No, the building that had once occupied this spot was long and perfectly rectangular, more like a municipal building than something you would normally find in the countryside.

26.

When she came back on to the lawn at Peacehaven her phone bleated as it received an answerphone message.

It was Victor, her boss. She called him back before going indoors.

'Just thought I'd call to see how you are?' he said.

'I'm fine. I'm having a break on the Gower peninsula.' She decided not to elaborate.

'Oh, lovely. Used to go there with my hubby. Three Cliffs Bay.'

'I've only just arrived, so haven't seen much yet.'

'Make sure you go there. And don't miss Oxwich – and of course Rhossili.'

'I will. How's the salvage op going?'

'Well enough,' said Victor. 'They've recovered most of what they can. Now it's a case of cleaning and restoring, and planning the stabilisation works. But there is one other thing I can tell you.'

'What's that?'

'They have ruled out – completely – the possibility of the fire being started by a fault in the distribution board.

It was hardly damaged. The electricians even managed to get it working again, without changing any parts. There's a small possibility it was a problem elsewhere in the wiring. But apparently that really is very unlikely.'

'So their next best guess is?'

'There isn't one at the moment. They've completely drawn a blank.'

'Another of Farthingbridge's mysteries,' said Alice.

'Yes,' said Victor.

'Any more news about Femi?'

'Oh yes, there's some good news there. She was semi-conscious for a few hours last week. They're fairly confident she's going to make a recovery.'

'That's good,' said Alice. She felt as if she could cry with joy – which was strange, as she barely knew the woman. What was it with her emotions these days? They were in shreds.

'But Mike's not so good,' said Victor.

'Oh?'

'No. He's been redeployed to Haverstone, but apparently he's had to take time off there. He's been acting a little strangely, according to the Property Manager.'

'In what way?' Alice thought that didn't sound like Mike at all, he was practically the most stable bloke she knew.

'Mainly time keeping. Being late in most days, not turning up for meetings. But – between you and me – he's also been saying some strange things to the gardeners there. Stuff about whether the house haunted or not. He seems to have become a bit obsessed by ghosts all of a sudden. And he seems to feel guilty about you.'

'About me?' said Alice, feeling exposed. All of a sudden she wanted to speak to Mike again, but knew that would have to wait. 'That's strange,' she said. 'He got the stepladder. He was trying to save me.'

'Yes. But maybe he thinks he could have done more, perhaps propped the ladder better to stop it tipping or something. It's funny how people's minds process traumatic events in the aftermath.'

'Yes,' said Alice. She remembered, almost physically, the sensation of the ladder moving before it fell. The competition of forces, how she had tried to manage them. Now she thought about it, it was almost as if there had been some kind of push from below. But that didn't make sense, Harry and Mike were holding it tight all the time. It was just the softness of the soil.

'Anyway, I'm afraid I've got to go,' said Victor hurriedly. 'Just realised I was meant to be in a meeting with James Houghton ten minutes ago.'

After they'd finished, Alice thought about what Victor had said about the distribution board. Then she thought about the figure that had appeared in the corridor and come through into the Drawing room. The burning man. Who was he?

Perhaps it was possible for a ghost to start a fire? Was she being blinkered in thinking ghosts could only ever act as they had done in her previous encounters with them? After all, this was the afterlife she was talking about. Impossibly mysterious, completely unknown.

What did she know about it? What could she ever know?

27

It wasn't until after eleven that Susannah had finished clearing the breakfast and tidying the house. Gareth had finally risen and was sitting with Jacob on his knee in the kitchen, reading him picture books.

'Coffee?' the blonde woman suggested. They took it out on the terrace, where they had eaten dinner the night before.

Alice told her about the phone call from her boss and the ongoing mystery of how the fire had started.

'I saw ghosts there, too,' she finished.

'Ghosts plural?' said Susannah.

'Yes. There's a young girl there who I've seen several times. A teenager. She was killed – likely killed – by a nineteenth-century libertine – a nasty little sadist, in fact – who owned the house. The second Lord Ashford. He was a monster.'

'What did he do?'

'Held a lot of wild, debauched parties,' said Alice. 'Abused the women in his life, as I'm sure he abused this Belgian girl, Eloise. He's believed to have murdered her, possibly in the Summer House. Her ripped and bloody dress was found in the woods nearby after she disappeared. But her body was never found, so he got away with it.' She looked at Susannah. 'I have this thing… when I get close to ghosts, sometimes, I can feel what they feel.'

'Can you?' said Susannah, her eyes wide.

'Yes. I came close to the girl and all I could feel was her terror. I'd never known anything like it.'

Susannah surprised her by drawing out a packet of cigarettes.

'I didn't know you smoked,' said Alice.

'I don't. I gave up before Jacob was born. But every now and then…'

She lit up and took a long, deep drag, staring off into the woods.

Alice felt butterflies in her stomach as she steeled herself to bring up the subject that had been a taboo for so long. 'Tell me what happened when Charlotte's grandmother attacked you like that.'

'A no-nonsense question, delivered in a no-nonsense way,' said Susannah, with a pinched smile.

'That's right. It's time for you to come clean, Susannah. Tell me why you turned on me. On us. And then what happened with the ghost. It might even help me to help you now. The more I find out about ghosts, the better chance I have of understanding them. So come on. Tell me why you did what you did.'

Susannah sucked on her cigarette again. 'I'm surprised you haven't guessed,' she said. She looked at her and waited.

'What?' said Alice. For a moment she felt all the conflicts surge again like a whipped-up wasps' nest. She felt like swearing but checked herself.

'Anger? Did I do something wrong?' she said.

'No. You never did anything wrong.'

'You're not going to tell me that was the problem?' Rage flashed again in her mind. For the first time she could understand what people meant when they said they saw red. Which wasn't like her at all. She'd never realised quite how much emotion she must have tucked away.

Susannah's face twitched, perhaps to stop a sneer. 'I was much more immature than I looked. I was in awe of you. You were so perfect. You knew so many things, read such cool books, articulated leftfield viewpoints with wit and intelligence. I'd never come across – no one had ever come across anyone like…' She trailed off.

'What?' said Alice. That didn't sound like her at all.

'After a while, I felt overwhelmed by you. I thought I was nothing compared to you, a no one. The smoking idea just popped into my mind one day and I went with it.'

'So it was spite?' said Alice, remembering how Susannah had lied about her smoking to her favourite teacher.

'Jealousy, I suppose,' said Susannah. She looked down, blew smoke at the ground.

'Jealousy?' said Alice. 'But I was jealous of you! You were so beautiful, you turned everyone's head. Plus you were smart as a tack. I was jealous of you.'

Susannah sighed. 'Teenage girls, huh?' she said.

'I can't believe it,' said Alice. It felt like such a waste of their lives, all based on misunderstanding. Was Susannah telling the truth? There was no reason not to believe her.

'So what happened with the ghost?' she asked, as Susannah stubbed out her cigarette with the edge of her shoe, then popped the butt into her mug.

'You tell me,' said Susannah tartly, looking down at the cup. 'You probably got a better view than me.'

For a moment Alice was reminded of the girl at school – the nasty version.

'No,' Susannah continued quickly. 'I – I don't know. To be honest, the last thing I remember was being so terrified as she came up to me that I actually wet myself. I don't remember what she did after that. I must have suppressed it. Successfully.'

'But you remember after?' said Alice.

'Yes. I was filled with dread. It was like falling down the biggest, emptiest hole, right in the centre of my brain. I panicked and had to get away. I couldn't remember ever having needed my mum before. But I needed her then.'

'It was a strange – *intervention*,' said Alice. 'I've thought about it a lot. I feel like it was wrong, too. Sure, you'd been mean as hell but that – that was way over the top.'

Susannah huffed, halfway to a laugh. 'You can say that again,' she said. 'I deserved some kind of punishment. But not that. No way that.'

'I agree,' said Alice.

'So now I've told you why I did it – is it time for the big question?' said Susannah.

'Yes, I suppose it is,' said Alice. She still didn't know whether she could one-hundred-percent trust her old friend – gaunt, harrowed, still striking – looking at her now across this ceramic table.

'Will you help us?'

28.

'Oh you!'

They turned to see Jacob standing up against the French door windows with both hands splayed against the glass. His hips swayed back and forth erratically as he grinned at them.

'Hello my lovely boy,' said Susannah, as he pushed himself off from the glass and began to trundle towards them. Gareth appeared behind him, coughing as he crossed the decking.

'Come to mummy!'

The little boy staggered across the decking towards her open arms.

'Of course I'll help you,' said Alice, quietly.

Susannah smiled at her and picked up the toddler. Elevated, Jacob swung round and pointed at Alice.

'Oh you!' he said again.

'What me?' she said, moving her face close to his.

He giggled and smeared her nose with the yoghurt that caked his fingers.

'Sorry about that,' said Gareth. 'I tried to clean him up before he came out.'

'No worries.'

Then Jacob's joyous expression fell away. He looked down and began to speak quietly to himself, a nonsensical babble.

'What's wrong?' said Susannah. 'Come on, honey, talk to mummy.'

But she couldn't get through to him. He was lost to whatever concern had overtaken him.

'Tell me about the other people you've had in – the ones who have tried to help,' said Alice.

'After the incident with Molly, we tried the local priest,' said Susannah.

'The Reverend Ferrari,' said Gareth with sudden relish and Alice realised how attractive he could be. 'One of the few Italian priests in the Church in Wales. Knew him since I was knee-high to a grasshopper. Dad used to have a beer with him in The Ship once in a while.'

'Nice as he was, he was bloody useless,' Susannah continued. 'Brought some holy water and traipsed around the rooms with a candle doing his "blessings". I asked him if he could do an exorcism but apparently there are very high bars to jump to even get the Church to assess whether one is needed. He told us we wouldn't have a chance, especially as there was no possession.'

'Except by terror,' Gareth muttered, returned to his normal self.

'After that, we did a lot of web search about parapsychologists or paranormal investigators or ghost hunters or whatever you want to bloody call them,' said Susannah. 'There were a few who were well-reviewed. A couple came over from Pembroke, an old woman and her forty-something son, they had all this equipment, infrared thermometers and a Geiger counter and stuff, which they set up all over the place. Things showed up, but there was stuff everywhere, a kind of background electro-magnetic activity which helped us precisely not-at-all. They went away all chatty and smiley with their two-hundred-quid fee.'

'That guy from Ross-on-Wye was helpful,' said Gareth. 'He was more into asking questions, doing research.'

'Yes, but at the end of the day all he really told us was that there was a smallpox hospital on our doorstep, pulled down forty years ago.'

'I think I saw that,' said Alice. 'When I was walking in the woods this morning. Up the hillside, through the pine trees?'

'Yeah, that's it,' said Gareth. 'You saw the foundations, did you?'

'Yes, brickwork. It's all overgrown.'

He nodded.

'Did it have a lot of patients?'

'Unlikely. There was an epidemic in the Valleys in the sixties, and for a while people were very worried. But I'm not sure it even saw a single patient.'

29.

In the afternoon, Susannah took Alice and Jacob up the coast in the Mercedes.

It wasn't long before they reached Three Cliffs Bay with its sea cliffs piled in a row at the western edge of the wind-swept beach, like the spines of a buried lizard. They parked and walked down the beach, alongside the stream that meandered through it like an ice cream swirl. Susannah had brought a kite, but Jacob was not at all interested in flying it. He was however obsessed by the qualities of the silk, which he finally managed to rip.

'So much for that,' said Susannah, stuffing the ruined kite into her backpack.

They took off their shoes and paddled amidst the families enjoying the good weather, splashing and trying out lilos and paddle boards. For a while Jacob took an intense interest in Alice (or *you*, as he continued to call her) and she struggled to make toddler-friendly expressions and play games that didn't come naturally at all. Still, Jacob didn't seem to mind. He kept flinging his arms around her, reaching up and appearing to want her to pick him up.

'You! You!' he shouted, grabbing the back of her neck.

She laughed, lifting him up for a moment as, with a surprising strong grip, he attached himself to her and looked over her shoulder at the sea.

'You!'

'Yes, me,' she said, laughing.

Later they drove on to Oxwich bay, another stunning stretch of unspoilt beach in between low wooded headlands. Sand dunes fringed the long beach, petering out into more woodland. Alice couldn't believe how beautiful it was, like something out of a travel brochure, perhaps from the Algarve or Caribbean. They walked down the beach and had tea and cake in the hotel at the far end of the bay.

'I love it here,' Alice said to Susannah.

'Yes. This bit is a dream,' said Susannah, forking a slice of lemon cake into her month as she sandwiched Jacob between her knees. The toddler sprawled over backwards to gaze upside down at the sea. Susannah said: 'So did that mind meld *thing* you described help you to get rid of the ghosts in that country house? I read that guy's blog, but I'm not sure I really understood it.'

'Yes,' said Alice. 'But it wasn't quite *get rid* of them.'

'No, cross over, I think you called it.'

'That's right. It suits it better. They had strong reasons for being there. One night I decided to just… walk *into* the woman spirit. It's hard to describe it, but I gained a sense of what had gone wrong for her, it was like living one of her memories. It threw a lot of light into what had happened, the crux of what was keeping her back.'

'OK,' said Susannah, slowly. Her face creased into a worried frown. 'So – if you manage to help us – do you think *that* might be how you do it? Do you think you'll somehow understand the ghost's raison d'être and help him to cross over?'

'Possibly,' said Alice. 'I really don't know. Some parapsychologists argue that's how it works. Films and books sometimes show that. And I have experience of it working once. But really, who knows?'

They were quiet for a moment as Susannah hoisted Jacob back upright on to her knee. He rested his head against her chest and watched Alice.

'What about old ghosts?' Susannah asked. 'That girl you talked about in Farthingbridge. How could you ever help an old ghost to cross over? There can't be any justice when the killer has been dead for hundreds of years, can there?'

Alice sighed. 'Who knows?' she repeated. 'Perhaps by someone understanding something, proving something, setting the record straight in some arena, public or otherwise. It's all a total mystery. There's no evidence for anything at all, it's all conjecture.'

Susannah squinted out across the sunlit bay. 'Yes,' she said. 'But you and I – we *know* they exist.'

Alice stared at her. 'Yes,' she said. 'We do. And there's something else I need to tell you. Now that I've agreed to help you.'

'What's that?'

Alice wondered whether Susannah's grimace was from staring too much at the bright sea – or from nerves. 'The guy who wrote the blog – Aitor Elizondo. The Basque. He's the guest you've got booked in tomorrow.'

'Oh,' said Susannah.

'Mummy, cake,' said Jacob. She took a spoonful of the lemon cake and slipped it into his gaping mouth.

'He's a fantastic paranormal investigator,' said Alice, seeing Susannah's uncertainty. 'Not like your normal amateur enthusiast. I think he will help.'

'You could have told me before.'

Again, Alice had a sudden urge to slap her. What was getting into her these days? Don't lose the upper hand, she thought. Remember she's the one who needs you.

'I think he will help,' she said again, her lips pinching at the corners.

'OK,' said Susannah. 'No, thanks, sorry,' she added. 'I'm sure he'll be useful. I'm just not so good with surprises.'

'*De nada*,' said Alice.

30.

'What's going on?' said Susannah under her breath, slowing the car.

Alice was checking her phone as they turned off the main road and headed up the gravel drive to Peacehaven. She looked up and saw that, straight ahead of them, half blocking the drive where it swelled out into the courtyard, was a small blue car. One of its back doors was wide open. Alice heard noise, shouting, and looked towards the house.

'I've told you, you can bugger off back to Swansea!' It was Gareth, booming at five young people, two boys and three girls. Alice saw the big man striding towards the youngsters. Even from here, she could see his face was a frightening colour, angry red, almost purple.

'We've come all this way,' said one of the boys, a tall, gangly youth wearing a biker's jacket with white lettering on the back.

'Yeah, come on, what's the harm?' said a girl, short and stocky with red hair in a ponytail. 'Just a quick look.'

'Oh no, look at the guests…' said Susannah, fumbling with her door handle.

Alice looked up as she climbed out. She could see two faces watching from different windows on the first floor.

'What's the harm?' shouted Gareth. 'What's the bleeding harm…?'

Suddenly he turned back and snatched up a broom that was propped up in the shrub border.

'Shit,' said Alice.

She began to run towards the group with Susannah. Jacob sat singing to himself, blissfully unaware in the back seat.

'Watch out!' shouted the second young man, as Gareth held up the broom in both hands and advanced on them.

'Run!' shouted a girl, 'He's a nutter!' They all fled back towards their car.

'Gareth!' shouted Susannah, but he wasn't hearing, hadn't even seen her and Alice. With a garbled yell – more agony than anger, Alice thought later – Gareth rushed at the students, lifting the broom high in the air.

He was surprisingly fast for a man his size and soon he was bearing down on the slowest member of the party, the girl with the dyed hair. Alice watched in horror as he raised the broom even higher and for a split-second she thought that was it, he was going to hit her on the head. She saw the raw-faced panic on the girl's face as she sensed, heard him right behind her, her pudgy hands coming up to the sides of her head in some kind of fearful-protective gesture.

'Stop!' Alice screamed.

But he didn't. The broom swung high and then came down towards the girl but at the last moment, as Alice screeched again, Gareth twisted, bringing the broom down to the side of the girl. There was a thump as it struck the car, the passenger-side door. The girl dived in through the open door at the back. With another terrible cry, Gareth crashed down heavily on his back.

The young people continued shouting and screaming as one of the girls struggled to get the engine started.

'Wait a minute!'

Susannah was at the passenger door. Gareth was lying on the ground, swearing and wincing, the shaft of the broom across his left ankle. The boy in the biker jacket cowered from Susannah in the passenger seat.

'Turn the engine off!' Susannah shouted. 'He's not going to do anything, he's hurt!'

'Ignore her, just get it going, Annie,' shouted the boy.

'I'm trying, I'm trying!' said the dark-haired girl in the driver seat.

'He's pulled his back or something!' said Alice, coming up alongside them.

The boy looked at her and Susannah. 'Has he?' he said.

The girl switched off the ignition and there was a moment's silence before Gareth groaned again.

'Ah my… ah, my effing back!' he said.

Alice kneeled down beside Gareth. He was gritting his teeth, spittle at the corners of his lips.

'What's wrong with him?' said the boy in the passenger seat.

'Is it seized?' said Alice.

'Yes,' Gareth gasped. 'Like someone stuck a bloody knife in – no, a hatchet.'

'Don't move,' she said. She looked at Susannah. 'I think we're going to need an ambulance.'

'An ambulance?' said Susannah. She glanced up at the house. There were a couple of men, one middle-aged, athletic, the other younger, bearded, coming out of the front door.

Alice stood up, took her phone out of her pocket, and dialled 999.

31.

It took over forty minutes for the ambulance to arrive. While they were waiting, Susannah stayed with Gareth whilst Alice spoke quietly to the guests, reassuring them that everything was in hand. She then collected Jacob from the car and took him over to the five young people, now standing awkwardly at a short distance from Gareth and Susannah.

'Oh, he's cute, isn't he?' said the girl with the ponytail.

'What were you doing here?' said Alice.

'We'd been down the beach and decided to come and have a look at the haunted hotel,' said one of the boys.

'Haunted hotel?' said Alice, staring at him. He had tortoiseshell glasses, a sharply elevated, already greying quiff, and sun-pinked skin.

'Yes, this place is all over the net,' said the boy in the black jacket. 'We just wanted a look.'

'See if we could see that ghost with the scary eyes,' said the driver.

'It's not a hotel,' said Alice.

Jacob, staring at the girl with the red hair, repeated: 'Otel.'

'It's not even open to the public,' said Alice. 'It's a guest house. You can only come in here with a reservation. It's these people's livelihood, not a bloody theme park.'

'OK,' said the boy with glasses. He looked at Alice and realised it wasn't enough. 'Sorry,' he muttered.

'Sorry?' repeated the girl who was the driver. 'He could have really hurt Mags!'

'Well he didn't,' said Alice. She looked at the car door. 'He just gave you a little dent. He's been under a lot of pressure. You shouldn't have been here, and you shouldn't have pushed him when he told you to leave. Where have you come from anyway?'

'Swansea,' said the girl who hadn't spoken. She was small and pretty, in a yellow T-shirt with a surf-board shaped print of sea spray on it.

'The university?' said Alice.

'You!' said Jacob. 'Daddy!'

'Yes,' said the girl, sheepishly.

'They're not going to be happy about this,' said Alice. 'Maybe we should just leave it there.'

'What about the dent?' said the driver.

'Get it fixed, or tap it out yourself with a hammer,' said Alice. She sniffed. 'Have you been smoking?'

The girl looked embarrassed. 'No,' she said.

'Don't take me for a fool,' said Alice.

32.

'Looks like a bad sprain to me,' said the paramedic, a barrel-chested man wearing dark sunglasses and smelling of menthol. 'But he's in a lot of pain. We're going to take him in to get an X-ray, just to be safe.'

'Just one bloody thing after another,' Susannah muttered. She glanced at the back of the ambulance in which Gareth had now been loaded, after the two paramedics had put on a neck collar and carefully lifted him on to a stretcher.

'You sure you don't want the police involved?' said the paramedic.

Susannah shook her head. 'No,' she said.

The students had left, Alice had taken one of their numbers, but she was sure it was the last they'd see of them.

'You should go with him,' said Alice. 'I can put Jacob to bed.'

Susannah looked at her uncertainly. 'No, he can be a little blighter at bedtime.'

'How about you put him down and then, once he's asleep, you go on after. I can babysit.'

Susannah checked her watch. 'It is already past his bedtime. I could do it within half an hour. Or maybe an hour at tops. OK then. Thank you.'

Alice smiled. 'No problem,' she said, realising that for all her doubts and worries, there was something about a crisis that brought out the best in her. Was that weird?

33.

After she had put Jacob to bed, Susannah gave Alice her mobile number in case she or any of the guests needed it, then drove off to the hospital in Swansea.

Suddenly, Alice was alone in the house. The guests – the walkers from Swansea and the Valleys, all three of them men – had taken their cars out, presumably heading

4off to the local pubs for dinner. Alice took a tour, following each of the corridors to its end, peeking into rooms, getting a feel for the size of the place. She was still struck by how calm it felt, the apparent lack of any ghostly friction. It was just… a normal guest house. She returned to the living room and sat on the sumptuous sofa in front of the fireplace with a book.

But instead of opening it she felt the force of the sudden peace and sat still, looking around at the room. The décor was tasteful, with a beautiful leaves-and-berries wallpaper on a dark, purple-black background. There were only three large paintings, all minimalist, low-colour seascapes. A vintage carriage clock ticked away soporifically on the mantelpiece. In the fireplace, peacock feathers stood in a thick crystal vase, with neatly stacked logs behind them.

Alice sighed and slumped into the corner of the sofa. Evening sunlight was warming her face, slanting brightness across the floorboards and pink-and-purple shagpile rugs. She opened her book, a Trollope, and began to read.

After a few minutes, her eyes began to droop. She realised that, after all the intensity of the last twenty-four hours, she was shattered. But it was too early to go to bed, wasn't it?

Eight-twenty. It certainly was. She considered switching on the TV but decided against it. Sure to send her to sleep. Her phone bleated and she saw a message from Aitor.

See you tomorrow, arriving c.4.30

After Susannah had done her part of the deal – owning up as to why she had treated her so badly – Alice had called Aitor to confirm that she was staying and he could come down for the weekend.

She texted him back a thumbs-up. Momentarily, she remembered the mysterious messages she'd received from her mum in Bramley. She thought about her mum's face, her aging face, how the skin had thickened around her lower cheeks and mouth, her lips almost vanishing, but how her greeny-grey eyes had remained serene, strangely more so as the dementia took hold. That untroubled gaze to the horizon. How she missed her…

Alice stood up and wandered off to make herself some tea. As she stood there, staring out of the French windows at the terrace and listening to the scorching of water, she heard a car pull up in the drive. Shortly after, as the kettle button clacked, the front door opened and someone walked through the hall, turned and climbed the stairs.

As there was only one set of footsteps she guessed it must be the man from the Valleys, Jo his name was. She'd only talked to him briefly during the incident with Gareth and the students but he was a nice chap, late forties, energetic, manager of a climbing centre. She thought about seeing if he wanted a drink, but he was bounding up the steps so she let him go.

The tea did the job of keeping her awake for another hour, during which the other two guests came back in their car. One of them, a young, bearded man with a thin face and sallow skin popped his head in to ask how Gareth was and she told him that she'd not heard any more, but suspected a torn ligament or slipped disc.

'If there's anything we can do to help, just let us know,' he said.

34.

At 9.30 she gave up and decided to take her book and Jacob's monitor up to bed with her. She detoured via the little boy's room – the monitor had been deathly quiet – and found him sound asleep in his crib, toy ducks and penguins and bears all piled around him.

As she headed back down the landing she saw a movement ahead of her and looked up, thinking it must be one of the guests.

But it wasn't.

It was him. The ghost.

He was about ten feet away, standing in the doorway of the bathroom, staring at her with awful, wretched eyes. Lit faintly, by his own inner light.

Alice drew in a sharp breath in shock and tried to take in as much as possible.

He was a tall man, wearing a brown suit of soft material, possibly moleskin, although that could just be his ghostly haziness. His shirt was white, with thin stripes, cufflinked at the sleeves. Stylish tan brogues. Enough of the clothes, his face – terrible. Very pale, something oddly mottled about it, hints of purple, yellow, even greenish in places – but no dirt. Tongue thick and protruding from the corner of his mouth, quivering, less pink than cream coloured. Narrow nose – very narrow – hair swept back, pale blond, thinning, especially at the temples, but he wasn't old, perhaps thirty-odd. But the eyes, God, the eyes…

They were coming out of his head, she was sure. She thought of the Hungarian actor, Peter Lorre, who probably had the most bulging eyes she'd ever seen – but these were worse, much more pronounced. In fact, his whole face was bulging, swollen.

His neck – check his neck – above the pristine white collar – yes, some smudges of colour there, a little red, blue, yellow even?

The man swung his head awkwardly and began to walk towards her. Instinctively, Alice took a step back.

'Who are you?' she said.

He took another two, three steps forward. Quick – take it in – his suit, shirt – old or modern? Too classic to say, the shoes, could be 1920s, could be twenty-first century, no way of telling. Anything about him giving away his era?

One of his hands lifted, as if feeling for things in the air.

'Whoever you are, I will help you,' she said, forcing herself to remain steady, to stand her ground.

She could see trouble, the building up of frenzy, in his eyes. God, could they fall out of their sockets? He was only a few feet away from her, she could see the blood trails in his sclera, they were hardly white at all…

For a moment, she felt a weakness in her legs and worried that she would collapse. She meant to move forward, to walk straight into the man, to see what might happen – but he looked so ghastly, and what was he doing, he was reaching up towards her, towards her face, she could see his fine, possibly manicured nails, what was he going to do, it looked like he was planning to… what? Strangle her?

'I can help you,' she said loudly, and then she realised what the dreadful entity was doing, he was…She felt a bolt of ice down her back.

He was pointing at her.

35.

'Are you all right, Alice?'

'What!' She spun round, saw Jo standing in the door of his bedroom halfway down the corridor behind her.

Before answering, she swung her head back to check on the ghost – but he was gone.

'Did you see him?' she said.

'Who?' said the man, coming towards her.

'Oh – no one,' she said, remembering the Parry's situation.

'Who were you talking to?'

'Just been saying goodnight to the boy – to Jacob,' she said.

'Oh, OK,' said the man. He turned and looked back, towards Jacob's room, and frowned.

Alice felt her heart clumping about in her chest as if it were wearing hobnail boots. She couldn't think of anything else to say, to explain why she was talking. So she just kept quiet, finally managing a smile.

Jo's frown lifted and he raised his eyebrows. 'I'm a light sleeper, that's how I heard you,' he said. He waited a moment then, realising she wasn't going to say anything else, said: 'Well, goodnight then.'

He turned away, back into his room.

36.

Alone in the corridor, Alice took a deep breath.

She looked at her lightly bandaged hand and saw that it was shaking. She might have faith that ghosts were the good guys, but they sure as hell could still scare the wits out of her.

She went back in to check on Jacob, just to make sure that the ghost hadn't gone in there. Then, with some trepidation, she checked all the other parts of the house. But there was no sign of him.

Despite her morning resolution she went to the kitchen and found the half-finished bottle of wine from the previous night. She poured herself a large glass. She took it up to her room and wondered about calling someone – Susannah, or Aitor. But she didn't want to stress Susannah anymore, not after Gareth – and Aitor would be with her tomorrow.

She drank the wine and, still feeling a stiffness in her neck, took a couple of painkillers. Then she climbed into bed and tried to ignore the repeated, ghastly images of the suited man that lunged at her each time she was on the cusp of sleep.

Saturday

37.

The Burning Man is standing in the corner of the room, wanting her to know that it is the middle of the night, she is alone, and the house is on fire. She murmurs to him, wanting to wake up. He lifts both his arms, makes his charred fingers into pistols like a kid, and points them at her. His fingers jerk up ninety degrees, mimicking the recoil as he fires. Then he opens and closes them, as if converting them from a gun into a pair of scissors.

She realises that she is a girl again, not a twenty-nine-year-old woman. She laughs at the man, who is now covered in a thick coat of flame. She is covered in an embroidered lace bedspread, patterned like her grandma's doilies. It would be fun to play with him and she would but she really doesn't like him. At all.

And he doesn't like her. He advances on her, blazing, with fire and fury, and now she can see that the whole room has in an instant caught light and she shouts for Mike, for a carpenter, as she sees that the Burning Man's eyes are themselves alight, the corneas blistering, and then she screams as he leans over her and roars…

And then the scene changes and she is running, running barefoot through the woods, and ahead of her is a woman in a white bonnet, and she glances back and sees him, the man with the red hair – Ashford – running after her, coming closer and closer through the trees…

She wakes up, hoping she has stopped the scream before it leaves her throat.

What is it with these dreams?

38.

'I saw him last night.'

Susannah was on her knees, stuffing sheets into the washing machine in the utility room. Jacob was trying to pull them out. She looked up.

'Not the ghost?'

'Yes,' said Alice.

'Oh my God. Where?'

'I'd just checked on Jacob and was going up to bed. He was on the landing. He was coming towards me. I tried to speak to him.'

'What happened?' Susannah stood up.

'Nothing. Jo heard me talking and opened his door to ask if I was all right. When I looked back the man was gone.'

'Did Jo see him?'

'No.'

Susannah pushed her hair away from her face. 'What did you think of him?'

'I'm no expert on these things. But I would say he was hanged.'

Susannah's nose wrinkled. 'I – I suspected as much. From people's descriptions.'

'Yes, he had marks round his neck, probably bruising.'

'Yuck. But you didn't – you didn't have a chance to help him… cross over?'

'No.'

'You might not get to see him again.'

'Who knows? Look, Aitor – when he gets down later – he will help me.'

'How?'

'I don't know exactly. But he's got some of the equipment. Ghost detection stuff. And he's sharp. He's good on research. He will help me – us – to work it out. If anyone can. But I've never done anything like this before. So I don't know. I think it's important to say you shouldn't get your hopes up. It's very possible that – well, that we might not be able to help you at all. You have to be prepared.'

Susannah stared blankly into space. Alice looked at her, wondering how much this house was rekindling her pain, the memory of Charlotte's gran.

'I adore you for trying, Alice,' said Susannah, with a half-smile.

Alice felt a surprising shiver of happiness. For a moment, it was like looking at the young girl who was her best friend, who she'd loved. A moment when all fresh potential was ahead of them.

Alice smiled and stared into Susannah's coral-green eyes. Only yesterday she'd been harbouring an irrational desire to hit her. How things changed. She was aware of Jacob near their feet, stoically continuing with his self-appointed task to remove all the sheets from the washing machine.

'How's Gareth?' she said, realising she should have asked that even before talking about the ghost.

'He's torn some ligaments in his lower back. Severely. He's going to need some physio and they've said he should use crutches for the first few days.'

'Have you brought him back?'

'No, they're going to keep him in, they had a bed and they're going to do some heat treatment and give him the drugs he needs for a couple of days. I'm picking him up on Monday.'

'Is it the stress, do you think?'

'Yes,' said Susannah. 'Apparently a guy turned up earlier yesterday from one of our catering suppliers, a local farm that gives us our pork, bacon and sausages, and Gareth got into a bit of a spat with him. He'd started off all nicey-nicey about our late payment, but then got increasingly threatening, talking about the recession coming. Gareth said he wanted to push his button nose up his face.'

'But he didn't?' said Alice.

'No. He sent him away with a partial cash payment, and a promise to settle by the end of the month. Then, a few hours later, the students arrived…'

'He blew a fuse.'

Susannah nodded.

'Whoopsy-daisy, Mummy,' said Jacob. They looked down and saw him standing happily on the mess of sheets.

'Yes, darling,' said Susannah.

39.

Susannah offered to take her to the end of the peninsula, to Rhossili beach, but Alice said she was just as happy to grab a towel and make her way down to the local cove and swim there.

The beach beneath the cliffs was stony but Alice was used to that – her parents used to take her down to

Brighton or Eastbourne when the weather got blistering hot. She changed into her swimming costume and entered the surprisingly warm – or at least, warm by British standards – water. She swam out a good way and then lay on her back, glancing at the cliffs as water snatched at her ears, watching the sky.

Beautiful.

She went into a relaxed, half-aware reverie. The tension and pain that had drilled deep into her neck and upper back over the last few weeks – ever since the fire, really – felt like it was seeping away into the healing sea. All her cares, the murderous people, ghosts, the sad loss of her parents, went. She would stay here like this, in some kind of mid-state, alone, perfectly afloat, forever.

She lost track of time. Then suddenly her bliss was shattered by a whooshing sound close by, a disturbance in the water, and she twisted and powered herself upright, treading water and staring about in the direction of the splashing. Was it a fish, or – surely not – a shark? She knew that there were basking sharks, giant plankton eaters, off the coast. Not man-eaters, but a graze with their skin would do some damage.

It took a moment to process the grey lump bobbing in the water some ten feet or so away.

Eyes. Puppy-dog eyes, brown. Eyelashes, a whiskery nose.

A seal!

The hammering in her chest, the momentary panic, transformed into wonder. A seal, looking at her with curiosity, out at sea. How brilliant!

Alice had heard of such encounters, but not known anyone who had experienced one first-hand. She stayed there for a while, watching the seal, while it watched her.

'Hello,' she said, smiling.

Its nose was dancing from side to side, as if in friendly acknowledgement. But more likely just countering the eddy of the waves, she realised.

'You're a handsome thing, aren't you?'

And then with a mighty twist, which sent a powerful current of water against her making her realise just how big the animal was, it was under the water and gone.

Feeling immensely cheered by the encounter, Alice swam back to shore.

40.

She sunbathed on the pebbles, listening to her music through earbuds.

For a while, she must have slept. She opened her eyes and stared at the pale sky through sunglasses. Her mouth was dry and she leaned up to take a swig of water from her bottle. Gulls were bobbing on the green sea, just a few metres out. Alice checked her watch: 1:25. She was hungry, but hadn't brought anything to eat. She decided to head back up to the house, make herself a sandwich. Then she would sit in the garden and wait for Aitor.

Glancing across the beach and at the steps that led up from the cove, she saw there was no one around so quickly changed out of her costume back into her shorts and T-shirt. She wrapped her costume up in the towel, popped on her sandals, and headed up the rickety wooden steps. For the first time in ages, she was feeling really good. It must have been the seal.

As she reached the top where the trees began she stopped, hearing a distant rumble. She thought it might be the same thing she'd heard yesterday, maybe a motorbike passing on the main road. She followed the path into the sunny pines, waving away a few flies that had evidently found something unpleasant near the path to feast on.

The engine noise went up an octave, revving.

She wondered if people did off-trail biking in these woods. Young men, out for an adrenalin hit on the weekend. Or more likely middle-aged men, trying to ignite some of their failing testosterone.

Whoever it was, they were coming into the forest. The burr of the engine increased, then waned, then revved ferociously, maybe a few hundred metres away. She was in another laurel patch, so visibility wasn't good. She began to feel apprehensive, not wanting to come suddenly up against some barely controlled machine, an excited teenager or panicked man wrestling the handlebars to avoid someone they weren't expecting. It was hardly like this was a popular stretch of forest.

Besides that, the noise was obliterating the pleasure she'd been taking in the sunlit wood. She felt cross. What was it with men and machines? Then she checked herself. Could be a woman.

When she reached the fork in the path she decided to take a detour, left up into the piney area, away from the bike – or bikes – up towards the octagonal shelter. Maybe she could wait there until they were gone.

'Blah!' she exclaimed, as another squadron of flies swooped in around her. Was it her towel, maybe the salt or sweat on her skin? She swiped at them hopelessly, but within a few strides they had cleared with the breeze.

The revving abated as Alice sweated her way up the path, past the place of the old hospital foundations. A pine needle jabbed against the side of her exposed toe. She was hot.

And there it was back again, coming fast towards her through the woods. Was she on private land? Susannah hadn't said anything about the woods being private property. Alice had just assumed it was public access. Maybe it was some irate landowner? Perhaps he'd spotted her from a clearing higher up and was intent on catching her and giving her a good telling off.

It was getting louder, the peace of the forest was shattered. She wondered about taking another diversion as the bike seemed to be coming from ahead of her, perhaps bouncing down the same cliff-edge path. It certainly sounded speedy, and she thought about her time in the Trust for England, witnessing scramble bikes tearing chaotically along muddy paths, their riders struggling to stay on like cowboys at a rodeo. She could see the sea through the trees now, on her left as she headed upwards. She didn't want to meet whoever it was head-on. But there was no other path. She couldn't just run off into the woods. If it was private land that would make her look even more suspect. Surely the best thing was to carry on and just feign – or rather, explain – her ignorance if he caught her?

The bike was close now, she was suddenly disorientated and thought it might actually be somewhere off through the woods alongside her. She looked deep into the trees and – there – yes! – there was the rider, but not on a scrambler, on a quadbike. The dark helmet turned towards her, watched her for a moment through the pines, and then the bike veered diagonally towards her.

Alice was scared.

What was he doing? She was sure he wasn't on a path, he was finding his way through the scrub and trees. Did he want to cut her off? She thought about shouting to him, but with the roar of the engine knew he wouldn't hear.

Besides – he looked mean. And, with quick turns of his head, he looked intent – upon her.

She felt the intensity of the heat, of indecision, of fear. She panicked and began to head swiftly back down the path, keeping away from the slope that fell away to the cliff edge with its straggly trees.

Behind her the quadbike revved angrily.

She glanced over her shoulder and saw the bike clambering across the rocks and tree roots, lunging between its four points of balance before finally mounting on to the path and...

Turning down towards her.

Alice ran, away down the path. The heel of her sandal flipped up, trapped against itself, threatened to send her flying but after a couple of stumbled steps she was steady again, running away. Without thinking, she cast her towel away as the engine throbbed down the footpath behind her.

Another glance back.

The helmet was dark but the visor was clear, not tinted, and she could see a face. But that was it – just two eyes and a nose, any man's face. A face jerking with the motion of the bike on the path. She suddenly felt like prey, like she was being hunted. There was a bewildering panic, a rampant force, inside her. She had to ignore it, to try and... survive.

Did he want to kill her?

Fleetingly she thought of the start of *Brighton Rock*, Hale's certainty that they meant to kill him, of a B movie she'd seen where a bulldozer chased people down on an island, of those wildlife programmes where the seized prey finally gave up the ghost…

It was louder.

It was louder still. He was right behind her.

She lunged off the path, went down steeply towards the cliff, slipping on needles, going down on to her lower back, sliding towards the edge, at the last moment as she glimpsed the sea below her jamming a foot against a thin tree and stopping dead.

She looked back up to see the quadbike flick off the path and then – realising he could go on no further without the machine overbalancing, without losing control and plunging down the slope – the driver stopped. He leaped off his bike and took two giant steps down the bank.

'Stop!' Alice screamed, grabbing up a stone to defend herself.

41.

The man stopped dead when she screamed.

'Are – are you OK?' he said, pulling off his helmet, long brown hair falling down around his shoulders. He was in his mid-twenties, broad-shouldered and conventional looking.

'What do you mean am I OK?' Alice yelled from the ground. 'You were the one chasing me on that bloody thing. You could have killed me!' She felt like she couldn't get enough air in her chest, her lungs were paralysed, her belly shuddering.

'No, I was just… I saw you running and came over to help.'

'Stay away from me!' she shouted, as he took a couple of tentative steps down the bank, stretching out a hand, the sleeve of his leather jacket shrinking back. She noticed how pale his fingers were, pinky-pale and large, almost swollen. Behind him, the engine of the quadbike was still rumbling, like a maniac lost in thought. Or somehow collaborative, thought Alice, like a hunting hound made to sit and wait.

'Whoa, OK,' he said, spreading his fingers out. 'I was only trying to help.' He stepped back and stood on the level, beside his dark machine. He began to bite his lower lip.

Alice glanced at the fall to the sea, just a couple of feet below her, then back up at the man. What was… he seemed… what was going on?

She wiped her forehead, feeling bits of grit. She didn't want to stand up. Was he lulling her into a false sense of security? She imagined him clubbing her around the head and sending her skedaddling over the edge to her death.

'Why did you do that? Why did you come after me?' she said, still panting for breath. 'I heard you all the way through the forest, coming towards me.'

'But I wasn't doing that, coming after you,' he said, frowning and rubbing his neck. He shook his head, as if trying to clear it. 'Well, not until I thought you were in trouble for… whatever reason. I was just riding the tracks, having fun.'

'Where are you from?'

'From? Mumbles.'

'What do you do?'

'I… I work for a dealer. Ford. Sell cars.' He looked up, squinted in the sunlight coming through the pines. Alice could see his forehead and pink cheeks beaded with sweat.

'Are you here on your own?'

'Yeah – yeah.' Alice thought he looked uncertain. 'Look, sorry,' he continued, 'I really don't know what you're getting at. I come here every Saturday morning and do a circuit through the woods. When I saw you looking scared, making your way along the cliff edge, I got – I suppose I got – kind of worried, thought you might be in trouble or something. Or that you might be…'

'What?'

'Well…' His eyebrows raised and he said quickly, as if suddenly inspired: 'There was a suicide here once.'

Alice shook her head. This was unbelievable. Utterly unbelievable. He had been bearing down on her. But he seemed so genuine, like he really didn't believe he had.

'How about I call the police,' she said, fumbling in her pocket for her phone.

The man blanched. 'Why?' he said. And then added: 'All right – if you want.'

She looked at her phone, flicked the screen, prepared to dial. Then she stopped and looked back at him. He was standing there in his leathers, biting his lip again.

He didn't get where she was coming from at all, she thought. He was clearly confused. Perhaps he really believed he was trying to help her.

She slipped the phone back in her shorts and climbed shakily to her feet.

'I'm coming up,' she said. 'Would you stand on the other side of your bike and turn its engine off?'

He did as he was asked and she made her way back up to the path, keeping the quadbike between them. Her thighs were weak and her mind was a storm of confusion, but her urge – almost incredibly – was to believe the young man. He was fresh-faced, almost naïve in appearance. And he looked a little… scared? He didn't match the stereotype of the random psycho at all.

As soon as she was on the level she took out her phone again and, before he could say anything, took photos of him and his bike.

'Are you going to the police?' he asked. 'Look…'

'I don't know,' she said. 'I haven't decided. Now tell me your name, phone number and address.'

'Andy Knight…' he began.

'Hold it!' she said, and turned her video on. She recorded him as he said:

'Andrew Knight.' He paused for a moment, as if struggling to remember, then continued: '0798668521, 43, Hartley Rd, Mumbles, SA3 4XZ. No – 4ZX. Jeez, my head…'

'Now say what you thought just happened.'

He gazed off uncertainly again, and then he turned at the camera and said: 'I brought my quadbike out here to the woods west of Caswell Bay for a scramble, like I do most Saturdays. I was riding around when I saw a woman – you – looking nervous and heading along the cliff edge path. I rode over to you and saw you running. I caught up with you when you stumbled off the path.'

'Why did you follow me?'

'I said, I thought you were in trouble. To be honest, I thought you might be intending to, like… take your own life, or something.'

'How do you think a woman feels if she sees a man coming towards her on a quadbike?'

'Well, scared, I guess. I would have got off and run, but it was the only way I thought I had of getting to you before… well, in case you were going to do something silly.'

'OK,' she said. She thought for a moment, biting her thumbnail. 'Have you been drinking – or taking drugs?'

He shook his head. 'What, at eleven o'clock on a Saturday morning?'

She looked at him expectantly.

'No. And I don't take drugs.'

'Have you been feeling OK lately?'

His dark eyebrows stretched upwards. 'How do you mean?'

'Anything unusual in your life?'

He shook his head slowly. 'No. No. Why do you ask?' 'Sure?'

'Yes. Although now you mention it, this has given me a splitting headache!' he winced and smiled weakly.

'OK,' she said. 'Take the keywha out of the ignition. I'm going to go get my towel and then I'm going to walk away down the path. I'm ready to call 999 with one touch. I don't want to hear you start the bike again for at least five minutes, right?'

'Look, I really wasn't…' he began.

'Five minutes – I'll be timing you!'

He gave a small nod. 'Right,' he said, stepping back up the slope to his quadbike. He pulled the key out and held it up in the palm of his hand, then slipped it into his pocket.

With a final, nervous glance at the man, Alice hurried off down the path.

42.

'Are you all right?'

It was starting to feel like Groundhog Day.

'Yes, kind of,' said Alice, coming across the lawn. Susannah was bent over, pushing Jacob across the grass on a red and blue toy tractor. The toddler was babbling happily behind the wheel.

'You look worried. You didn't see the ghost again, did you?'

'No. I just had a very odd thing happen in the woods, though. Upsetting.'

'What?' Susannah asked, standing up straight and putting a hand on Alice's shoulder.

'I'd been for a swim and was coming back through the forest when I heard what I first thought was a bike revving its engine. Soon this guy appeared on a quadbike, and he cut me off and began to come towards me on the path. I ran and tripped – I could have fallen over the edge of the cliff – but when he got to me I screamed at him and he froze. Then he acted all kind of confused, claiming he'd just been trying to help. Thought I was a jumper, or something. But he was pretty shaken.'

'Sounds like a nutter,' said Susannah. 'You must have been petrified. Did you call the police?'

'No, but I got his details. I was thinking of calling them when I got back here, but I'm not so sure now.'

'How weird.' Susannah turned a little, and looked up at the house.

'Too right. I just can't make sense of it. He seemed like a normal bloke, once he'd stopped. Helpful, even. It doesn't add up.'

'Nothing adds up round here,' said Susannah.

'Mummy push, push Mummy!' said Jacob, frustrated with his lack of progress. Susannah bent down and gave him a good run across the lawn. Jacob cooed his delight.

Alice checked her watch. 2.50. Aitor would be here in an hour and a half. She needed to see him more than ever.

'The quadbiker mentioned a suicide from the cliff,' she said. 'Did you know about it?'

Susannah stood up straight. 'No,' she said. 'First I've heard of it.'

There was the rising and falling plink of a xylophone, Susannah's mobile. She fished it out of her pocket. Alice played with Jacob while his mother talked.

'Hi hun, how are you?... yes… yes… oh no… oh no, poor you…yes…yes, she saw him! Saw him last night, while I was out with you… on the landing… yes, she tried but Jo heard her talking and came out… no, he doesn't know, she didn't say anything about it to him… don't worry, love… don't worry… she's got a friend coming soon, our booking, he's one of these paranormal investigators… no, I hope not –' she glanced briefly at Alice, looked away, before adding: 'He's the one whose blog I found, the way I found out about Alice again…yes… yes… you take care, I'll pick you up on Monday… bye.'

'How is he?' said Alice.

'Miserable,' said Susannah. 'His back is killing him, he says he can't move an inch without what he calls the *Night of the Long Knives.*'

'You didn't tell him about the quadbike?'

'No, didn't think of it. I suspect it was just a misunderstanding, don't you? I can't imagine he was really out to harm you.'

Alice pulled a face. 'I don't know,' she said. 'Perhaps he was trying to scare me or something…'

'Why would he?'

'I don't know.'

43.

'Darling!'

The swarthy young man with the bleached hair beamed out of the window of his yellow Renault as he drew to halt in front of the guest house. 'I've missed you!'

He switched off the engine and the car wobbled as he leaped out to embrace Alice.

'It's so good to see you again, Aitor,' she said, laughing. He always made her laugh.

'And who is this?' he said, reaching down to pick up Jacob, who was scrambling towards him with arms outstretched.

'Jacob,' said Susannah.

'Hello, my friend,' he said in his husky Spanish accent, as Jacob tackled his black stubble with pudgy fingers. 'You must be Susannah,' he said, craning his neck to look around the boy's blond curls.

'Yes. Pleased to meet you, Aitor. And thank you for providing a means for me to get in touch with my old… friend.'

Alice felt a stir of emotion in her gut. Pride…?

'I heard about your husband's injury,' said Aitor. 'How is he?'

'He's in hospital,' said Susannah. 'But he'll be out on Monday, if everything goes OK.'

Aitor nodded. 'Good,' he said.

'Would you like a drink?' said Susannah.

'What time is it little fellow?' he said, twisting his arm up behind Jacob to check his bulky analogue watch. Alice noticed at least four small dials within the dark blue face.

'Coffee time,' he said. 'I can set up the equipment before we have a proper drink. I have a good Porto in the trunk.'

'Daddy,' said Jacob.

Aitor chuckled. 'Not me,' he said.

'Lady,' said Jacob.

'Me?'

The boy swung around, at ease in Aitor's arms, and pointed at Alice. She wondered why it was that everything Susannah's little boy did and said seemed suggestive or ominous to her. No doubt about it, she'd watched one too many horror films.

44.

After coffee, Aitor set up his equipment all over the house. Alice followed him around, seeing him place his homemade devices in the hallways, Susannah and Jacob's rooms, and the Reading room. He had two large backpacks, in which Alice glimpsed a jumble of gadgetry, tablets, and cables, alongside a change of clothes and a leather wash bag.

'Does any of this stuff actually work?' asked Susannah, as they watched him mount a camera on a floating shelf opposite Jacob's cot.

Aitor looked at her. 'You want my honest answer?' he said.

'Yes.'

'In which case, yes,' he said. 'But it's a bit like what they say about advertising. Half the money is wasted, flushed away – but you can never say which half. But with ghost hunting, I'd say it's more like ninety-seven to ninety-eight percent of effort is wasted – but with the other two or three percent you just might find your ghost.'

'What do these things do?' said Susannah.

'Various. These that I'm putting up, I've made myself. This –' he held up an ordinary-looking video camera, '– will come on if something breaks the infrared beam and start recording. It may look cheap but it's *very* expensive by the way, it's a research camera, so be careful. But I've also connected it up to this –' he showed her a yellow, handheld tool, which was attached to the camera with a set of wires, 'which will measure any disturbance in the electromagnetic field as soon as the camera comes on. Or conversely, turn the camera on when it senses any change in the ambient EMF. This one here is for changes in temperature. And I use the tablets' video function too, but mainly they're here for the audio element as the expensive camera doesn't have audio. In case anything goes bump in the night!'

He laughed, but stopped when he saw Susannah's face.

'I know how much this means to you,' he said. 'Alice told me. I know the effect it has had on your family and on your livelihood. Believe me, I will do my best to see if I can help you find and hopefully understand this ghost.'

'How long have you been doing this?' said Susannah.

'Since I was a kid.'

'What started you?'

'We lived in Guernica.'

'In Spain?'

'The Basque country. Do you know what happened to Guernica in the Spanish Civil War?'

'No.'

'The Germans – with a little help from their Italian friends – bombed it from the air. They did it because they wanted to test out, what do they call it now – shock and awe. Yes, shock and awe. They killed thousands of civilians to try out a new type of warfare. With *El Caudillo* – General Franco's – consent, of course.'

'How disgusting!'

'Yes. Anyway, I was six years old when I saw one of the victims of the bombing. She was an old lady, a market woman. It was in broad daylight, and she was hurrying around, distressed and searching for something – or someone. I remember looking up at my parents, my brother, around at the crowds and the stallholders – expecting someone to do something. Maybe help her out. But no one did. Because no one else could see her. That was the start of my fascination with ghosts and the paranormal.' He smiled and added: 'It's lasted a long time.'

'Have you seen many?'

'Ghosts? No. No one has seen many ghosts. I think Alice has seen the most of all the people I've ever met and interviewed. At least, of all the people I've met and interviewed *and* believed. I have seen this market lady and one other, a teenage boy who drowned in a river near Oxford. His father hated him.'

'How intriguing, you must tell us more later. If you don't mind of course,' said Susannah, smiling.

Her charming smile, thought Alice. She remembered that charming smile well. And how Susannah could use it to wrap people around her finger.

45.

Whilst Susannah was putting Jacob to bed, Alice and Aitor sat out on the sunlit terrace, drinking some of Aitor's Portuguese wine. Alice described the encounter with the ghost in as much detail as she could.

When she had finished, Aitor sat back and whistled softly. 'Wow,' he said. 'You certainly have something, my friend. The amount of encounters you've had, it blows me away! They come to you like dogs to their mistress.'

'Great,' said Alice, rolling her eyes.

'It's good,' said Aitor. 'I know a hundred people who would kill to see just one of the ghosts you've seen.'

'Great,' said Alice again.

'Anyway, getting back to this one, it is very interesting,' said Aitor. 'I've been doing some research that I think might tie in with this ghost. There's nothing special about this place, Peacehaven, I think it was just a private home when it was built in the early twentieth century. But there's a few things on the net about the smallpox hospital. I have a friend who is a medical writer, he works for King's College London. I asked him if he could find anything about it through his sources. And he did. He found something intriguing.' Aitor spoke quickly, almost slurring his words in his enthusiasm – and in his second language.

'What?' Alice shaded her eyes against the sun, still high above the treetops.

'The hospital was built during an epidemic in 1962. Smallpox had already been eradicated once in the UK by a vaccination programme but someone went to Pakistan and brought it back again. There were outbreaks in Wales and England, mainly in the Valleys here. But there was only ever a handful of patients who used this hospital. Seven or eight, I think. The sad thing was, most of them died.'

'Were any of them men?'

'No, they were all children. But there was a doctor who was looking after them. He was a real character. All the children loved him. He pulled out all the stops to cheer them up, apparently. Dressed up as characters from children's books, put on funny accents, told stories, showered them with gifts. And the poor man couldn't take it when, one after the other, they began to die. He became depressed. He came back to the hospital on the day after the last one died – a seven-year-old boy – and hanged himself.'

'No!'

Aitor nodded.

'But that means it could be him, couldn't it?'

'Quite possibly. He looks like he was hanged, from what you say.'

'Wow. Poor man. But why would he be *here*, in Peacehaven? Wouldn't he be in the woods, where the hospital used to be?'

'Who knows. We have to catch him to find out. Our best hope is if you can do your mind-merge thing again. I've been having some thoughts about that, too.'

'But waitV a minute!' said Alice. 'I did have a creepy feeling that I was being watched in the woods the other day. Like there was someone behind me in the trees. I looked really hard – but I'm sure there wasn't anyone there.'

'Interesting,' said Aitor.

'Hi guys…'

They looked around as Susannah emerged from the kitchen doors. 'Everyone happy with lasagne?'

They both nodded.

'Have some *vino*, Susannah,' said Aitor. 'I'm happy to cook if you show me where everything is.'

'No, I couldn't possibly…'

'I love cooking, darling,' he said. 'Honestly.'

'He wouldn't offer if he didn't mean it,' said Alice. 'And he is an excellent cook.'

'Well – if you really don't mind, I feel like I've been run off my feet the last few days. There's ragu all prepared in the fridge, and fresh pasta sheets.'

'No problems. Alice can tell you all the things I've found out about the old hospital.'

46

'So tell me, Susannah, how did you come to live out here? Did you always want to run your own guest house?'

Aitor had cooked a delicious meal, which they had eaten as the sun went down over the trees, the distant swish of the sea growing louder with the darkness.

'Yes,' said Susannah, setting down her wine. 'I'd been running a stationery business in Cardiff for three years with a partner when I met Gareth. He was a hotel manager, but jaded with the corporate life. On our first date – he took me up Ystrad Mynach, to the dogs! – we were already plotting our dream life out here on the Gower, with our own place.'

'Running your own guest house sounds a bit more exciting than stationery,' said Aitor, chuckling.

'Hey, I used to spend hours in our village stationery shop when I was a kid!' said Alice.

'Yes,' said Susannah, smiling. 'People have a funny thing about stationery.'

'There's nothing like a new notebook with crisp white paper,' said Alice. Briefly she recalled an old, vague anxiety, about wanting to make sure the first thing she wrote in her new pad was something special – then always being disappointed.

Aitor smiled and looked back at Susannah. 'Did your partner – sorry, was he a boyfriend, or just a business partner? – carry on the business alone?' He wiped some of the béchamel sauce off his plate with a finger and licked it. Alice noticed a quick grimace appear on Susannah's face.

'Just a business partner – and how clever of you to guess that it was a man,' said the blonde woman, with a wry smile. 'And no, it was wound up when I left.'

The sky was now deep blue, making the candles in their fractured-glass globes come into their own. As Susannah drew back, Alice could see her expression change, a sudden hollowness, or shadow, in her eyes.

'And you invested the money from that into this place?' said Aitor, his dark eyes gleaming.

'Yes.'

Alice felt Susannah's discomfort. She was surprised at Aitor, talking about money like that. Perhaps they were more open about finances in the Basque country than here in the UK. Suddenly she remembered that, whilst she'd spent hours talking about the ghost to Aitor, she hadn't told him about the quadbike incident yet. She was about to break the momentary silence when he said:

'Alice, you haven't told me the details of the Farthingbridge fire.'

So she told him the story, starting with the reappearance of the girl in the ivory dress, then Femi falling from the gallery, the desperate attempt to save the collection, the ghost of the burning man – about whom Aitor wanted much more detail – and then her narrow escape from the second floor, on the perilous stepladder.

When she finished it was properly dark. Aitor whistled through clenched teeth.

'You are lucky to be alive, darling,' he said.

She nodded. 'Yes, thanks to Ben – and Harry and Mike.' Even as she said it she shuddered slightly, remembering the sudden lurch of the ladder and the horrific sensation as she fell backward.

Aitor nodded sagely. 'How long do they think it will be before the house reopens?'

'Eighteen months to two years, minimum. I think it'll be longer. Once it's safe they might do a partial reopening. People would probably be interested in seeing the extent of the damage.'

'They still haven't established the cause?'

'No. They thought it was the distribution board at first, but they've found there was nothing wrong with that.'

Aitor swilled his wine, then leaned forward on the table with his fingers on his lips.

'It's strange, for a ladder to tip like that,' he said. 'When someone is coming down. And someone's holding it.'

'Yes. But it was a stepladder and they'd had to prop it in the flower beds, which wasn't safe. I didn't have any choice but to go for it. There was no time, the flames were up against my back. And the air – even with the window open, it was unbreathable.'

Aitor stroked her shoulder. It was a gesture she would have felt uncomfortable with if he'd been British. 'Was Ben OK?' he said. 'He was the one who broke your fall, wasn't he?'

'Yes. I managed to smash a few of his ribs and his collarbone, though.'

'What job does he do?'

'He looks after the shop.'

'What about the guys holding the ladder?'

'Mike's the Head Gardener. Harry is his volunteer, an old chap.'

Aitor raised his eyebrows. 'Oh.'

Alice looked at him. 'What do you mean – oh?'

'Just a little surprised. People like that would be used to putting ladders up safely. Couldn't they have put it on the flagstones?'

'I wouldn't have been able to reach it. It was hard enough as it was. The platform was a good five foot below the window.'

'Wasn't there anything they could put under the feet to stabilise it?'

'I don't know,' she said. 'Not that I can think of.' Again she remembered the weird sensation of the forces as she tried to descend. 'Now you mention it though, there was – I don't know – it did feel a little like…'

'Yes?'

'It's silly, but it felt as if there was a bit of a… push from below. Sideways. I can't be sure…'

Aitor raised his eyebrows.

'What?' she said. 'What are you thinking?'

'Nothing,' he said. 'Just asking questions.'

'Mike and Harry have been with us for ages,' she said quickly. 'It's unthinkable that – well, why would they have done something like that?'

'It would only take one of them.'

'What are you saying?'

'Nothing, darling,' said Aitor hurriedly. 'Was there anyone else by the ladder?'

'I didn't really look. Yes – a few people were around. Flo. And Ben was a few metres away, obviously. I think there was somebody else too, possibly a member of the public, nearby,' said Alice, remembering the confusion, all those faces looking up at her intently.

Aitor nodded, then said: 'You broke your hand, didn't you?'

'Just a couple of fingers. They've healed well.' She stretched the fourth and fifth fingers on her bandaged hand to demonstrate. 'Lost a good millimetre off the top of my thumb, too,' she said, showing him the pale scar.

'But you're basically better now, that's good.'

'Yes,' said Alice. 'Although now you mention it, I have been taking a lot of painkillers recently. Headaches and a stiff neck.'

Aitor frowned. 'Maybe get it checked out, Alice. You might have suffered another injury in the fall that they didn't discover.'

'They did check me over pretty well in the hospital.'

'Still.'

'Maybe I will, after we've seen what we can do here,' said Alice, looking at Susannah.

'Yes, and after that we need to think about what we can do for this girl in Farthingbridge,' said Aitor. 'The girl in the ivory dress.'

'What – go back to Farthingbridge? That's not possible, the whole place is shut down.'

'Maybe when you're back in work. If they reopen it partially, like you say. She obviously needs something. And who knows about this burning man? The pair of them – they're an interesting puzzle.'

'Yes, his face,' she said, remembering with a shudder the tight brown skin, burnt eyes. And then remembering her nightmare. 'I've been dreaming about him. Or rather, having nightmares about him. And her, the girl,' she said. Aitor raised his eyebrows. 'But sheesh, it's late,' she added. 'I really need to go to bed, I'm so knackered.'

Susannah yawned. 'Me too,' she said.

'How about you, Aitor?' asked Alice.

The Basque smiled. 'Oh no. If you don't mind, I'll sit out here and finish this bottle of wine. I'm far too restless to sleep.'

47.

Alice would have liked another bath, but she was simply too tired.

She went to bed and fell straight into a deep slumber. But after what felt like just a few moments she was awake again. Wide awake, like she was sometimes when the first dead-to-the-world sleep of alcohol had worn off. But she hadn't drunk so heavily tonight.

She lay in bed thinking about the day. The questions Aitor had asked, the encounter with the seal, the flies and quadbike incident – damn, she still hadn't told Aitor about it! In the morning…

She turned on to her other side and saw the moonlight, turning the lily-patterned curtains to grey. Her neck was aching and her head hurt again. She was restless, out of sorts, and she suddenly realised it had something to do with… being watched.

She looked up into the dark corner of the room, where she could just make out the shape of the large, antique wardrobe. On top of that, unseen in the dark, was the contraption that Aitor had rigged up. Watching her. She imagined she had slept like a lump of rock for the past – she looked at the alarm clock – hour and a half – but from now on the recorder would probably be going on more as she tossed and turned through the hot night.

And it made her uncomfortable. She just didn't like being watched.

Sunday

48.

She is running, running through the woods, fast as she can and there, as she looks up ahead through the thin black rods of the trees, is a flash of grey, a white head, no, a white bonnet – someone else is running too and behind them there is someone following them, she can hear grunting, it's him, the red-haired man – Ashford! – she turns, to see the wild look in his hooded eyes – and she runs, runs faster, Ashford behind her, through the trees and there is the girl with the bonnet, ahead, they are both running, with Ashford some way behind them now and then the ground is descending, golden leaves are shushing around her naked feet, she is running down a slope towards a ditch and then she sees the girl ahead has fallen in the black ditch and is looking around, white, a look of horror in her eyes – oh, the horror, Ashford close behind – and she sees the girl in the ditch open her eyes wider and she is screeching, the girl is shrieking in the woods under the heavy autumn sky…

Alice opened her eyes.

Sunlight was filtering through the curtains, brightest on the white of the lilies. Her mouth was parched and her head felt like an iron bar had been implanted behind her eyes. She reached for the glass of water beside the bed and propped herself on an elbow to drink. She checked the clock: 6:49.

She had rarely felt so groggy. But she'd only drunk a couple of glasses of wine. She looked up at the dark block of the camera, this one camouflaged to catch wildlife outside, not ghosts indoors. Beside it sat its yellow plastic companion, the electromagnetic field reader.

Had anything happened during the night?

Twisting her head slowly, she eased out of bed. She felt like an old woman, all achy and fuzzy headed. She slipped on a T-shirt, shorts and pumps, and headed downstairs.

49.

In the kitchen she poured herself coffee, catching sight of the three guests already out on the terrace. Susannah was taking orders.

Alice went through into the sitting room and found Aitor sound asleep on the sofa. She diverted back to the kitchen and poured a black coffee, then took it through to him.

'Wake up, sleepy head.'

His head remained tipped back on the backrest of the sofa, mouth slightly open.

'Aitor – wake up.'

His eyes flicked open. He sat up and smiled, taking the coffee from her.

'Did you go to bed at all?' she said.

'No,' he said. 'I sat up waiting for the ghost. And surfing the web.'

'Presumably you didn't see him?'

'No. Unfortunately not.' He took a gulp of coffee and stood up. 'But now I'll go see if we've got anything on film from last night!'

He put his mug down on the table and ran off excitedly.

Alice smiled to herself and headed out on the terrace. The two young men from Cardiff were tucking into full English breakfasts, whilst Jo, the man who managed the climbing centre, was at a separate table drinking tea.

'Morning, love,' he said. 'You alone? Why don't you come and sit with me?'

'Sure, if you don't mind,' she said.

'I'd be honoured,' he said, in a broad Valleys accent.

'You're all up early,' she said, as she sat down opposite him.

'Oh, I never sleep well,' he said. 'Especially in the summer, when it's hot and the sun's up early.'

He sounded surprisingly cheerful, considering.

'Where have you come from?' he asked.

'Leamington.'

'Oh – Royal Leamington Spa,' he said, with a smile.

Alice nodded.

'The wife and I visited once. Lovely town. We were staying in Kenilworth.'

'Where you saw the castle?' she asked.

'Oh yes. Amazing. And Warwick Castle, too. What a beautiful part of the United Kingdom it is. Stratford-upon-Avon…'

'It's got its fair share of heritage, that's for sure,' said Alice.

'My wife loved it.' Alice noticed his eyes take on a sudden shine, before he said: 'So what brings you down to the Gower?'

'I'm a… friend – of Susannah's.'

'Lovely couple. Is Gareth all right – after that dreadful shower turned up yesterday? Pulled his back, didn't he?'

'Yes, I think he's coming home tomorrow.'

'Good, good. Have you managed to explore the area yet?'

'Yes, I've been up to Three Cliffs and Oxwich with Susannah and Jacob. And I've been walking around the woods and cliffs at the back.'

'These woods here?' he said, pointing his thumb over his back.

'Yes.'

'Did you see the foundations of the old hospital?'

Alice nodded, her curiosity piqued. 'You know about it?' she said.

'Well not much. But I've an interest in local history. That hospital was built for a smallpox epidemic in the nineteen-sixties.'

'Yes I've heard.'

'Only had a few patients – mostly kids – but a few died, sadly.'

'Yes. Someone mentioned a much-loved doctor who couldn't cope with it all and killed himself,' said Alice.

'Oh really? I didn't know that.'

Damn. She'd hoped he might.

'Did you know that this place was part of it too?' he asked.

'What?'

'Yes, Peacehaven. Before it was called Peacehaven of course. The NHS took on the lease when it was derelict. They were scared they were going to run out of beds and space to manage the patients. The new building was just beds – they practically threw it up! – and they used this building for administration and storage in the end. Staff rooms, that kind of thing.'

'Wow. That's interesting.'

They were interrupted by the two young men getting up from their table and saying goodbye to them.

'You leaving us, boys?' said Jo.

'Yes, back to work tomorrow,' said the scrawny man with the beard.

'Whereabouts?'

'Ponty.'

'My niece used to live on Pencerrig Street.'

'Yeah, I know.'

'Going anywhere on your way back?'

'Might stop off at the Forest Park.'

'Afan?'

'Yeah.'

'Enjoy, lads.'

50.

'Look – look at this!'

In Aitor's bedroom, sitting in a chair by the window, Alice watched him replay the video on his laptop, which was perched on a small table.

The infrared camera kicked into life, showing a large double bed with a black quilt and a woman twisted on her side, her white hair all around her on the pillow.

Susannah. At 1.32am.

After a moment, she rolled over on to her back, her eyes still closed. Then, as Alice watched the red seconds flash by, the woman lifted a knee up under the quilt, partly obscuring her face. Then the knee came down and the woman turned on to her other side. In her sleep, she began to stroke her hair. Moments later, she twisted back into her original position. Her mouth became black, open as she breathed deeper, or perhaps snored. Her eyes remained closed.

'Look – look here,' said Aitor, holding the yellow electromagnetic field reader up to her. The readings – one in V/m and the other in μt – were racing up from zero, the first into the low thousands, the second fluctuating between twelve and sixteen.

'What does that mean?' said Alice. 'I guess the first's volts per meter, but what's the other one?'

'Magnetic field,' said Aitor. 'And that's a high reading. Mobile phones and other electric devices can trigger it, but not to this level. And here –' he showed her a small digital clock that was wired between the two devices '– this told me the time of those EMF readings, which are the same as the camera's. I've rigged it up so the device kicks into life when it receives a signal from the camera. Because the camera is only likely to come on when there's significant movement.

'Look! Watch – watch…' he said, thrusting the laptop a little too close to Alice's face in his excitement.

Suddenly Susannah's hand shot out from beneath the cover, pushing away at the air. She rotated again, ending up stretched diagonally across the bed.

'How long does it go on for?' said Alice.

'About twenty minutes.'

'She doesn't wake up?'

'Not at all. Although I suspect she comes close to it, possibly in REM.'

'Do you think it's something to do with the ghost? Is he haunting her?'

'Who knows, darling? My hobby is all about guessing.'

'So, if you have to guess?'

'Yes. Absolutely, given the frequent sightings in this building, the history – this is a ghost. In my opinion.'

'Wow.'

'But – and this is a significant but – this is not all we've got to show from last night. There is something which is a little bit stranger.'

He looked at her significantly. 'Prepare yourself, Alice.'

51.

He shrunk the existing window and clicked a different file.

An image of another bed, another room, another sleeping figure appeared on the screen. The room was longer and there was a large floor-to-ceiling set of dimly-lit curtains across the window, which was built out from the slope of the roof.

Alice watched the figure shifting under the dark quilt. 'It's me,' she said.

Aitor nodded, his hand clasped across his mouth as he stared over her shoulder. Alice watched as she began to twist and turn under the covers, slow at first and then increasingly intense.

'It's like I'm doing some kind of dance,' she muttered. 'Or having a fit.'

'Yes, darling, yes. But watch – watch now!'

Suddenly, she sat bolt upright in bed, her eyes staring straight up at the camera.

'What the…' said Alice.

'Do you remember that?'

'No. Not at all.'

She remained in that position for a few seconds, her eyes locked on the device, then collapsed back on to the bed. She twisted once, twice, and then became still.

Despite her experience of the paranormal, Alice felt a slow dread grow from the deepest part of her gut, feeling its way up through her inner organs, making her lungs tight and her heart press quicker against what felt like a solid, gripping fist in her chest. She needed air, stood up and leaned out of Aitor's open window. She looked at the green lawn, at Susannah tidying the breakfast things on the terrace below.

She felt Aitor's hand on her shoulder.

'So freaky,' she whispered. 'Seeing yourself like that.'

'I'm here,' he said.

She looked around at him, saw his thin, sallow face with the dark stubble and near-black eyebrows, such a contrast to his soft, summer-straw hair.

'I'm here,' he said again, 'and I will help you.'

She nodded, stepping back into the room, and sitting down.

'He came up to see me, too…'

Aitor drew in breath. 'No, not quite.'

'What do you mean?'

'Look here,' he said. He showed her the EMF readings on a separate window.

'Similar to those in Susannah's room,' she said.

'Yes. Exactly. So, in my humble opinion, a ghost too.'

Alice nodded. 'I can sense an *and*…'

'Look here, Alice,' he said. 'Look at the time.'

Alice looked at the side of the screen.

'One-forty a.m.,' she said. 'But that means…'

'Yes. You were visited at exactly the same time as Susannah.'

She frowned. The fear was returning, slithering right up her spine now, coming like a cold eel into her brain.

'The ghost can be in two places at once?' she said.

'Or – there are two ghosts.'

52.

'There can't be…'

'Alice, I've been researching and exploring paranormal phenomena for seventeen years now, ever since I was an eleven-year-old boy. There are a few people who believe in bilocation, the capacity of a spirit to be in two places at the same time – some of them use the theories of quantum physics to back it up – but there's very few recorded experiences of it. Two ghosts – in my opinion – is far more likely.'

'But neither Susannah nor Gareth have mentioned other ghosts.'

Aitor shrugged. 'Maybe they don't know about this one.'

Alice stared at the screen. She felt again the terror of the unknown. She had never panicked when faced with the supernatural, always found that, despite the contradiction, there was a reason for ghosts being around, a rational explanation, if you like. But this felt more deeply sinister in some way, a secret presence visiting her at night while she slept. Her mind was full of half-formed questions, competing for space, leaving her overloaded, speechless.

'I – I'm stunned,' she said, shaking her head slowly. 'And scared.'

'And one more thing,' said Aitor. 'On this strange night.' He picked up a third camera from the bed and plugged it in.

Alice's thoughts raced. 'Not Jacob?' she said.

'No,' he said.

As soon as the video filled the screen Alice saw that it wasn't a bedroom at all, but the downstairs living room. And there, on the sofa, was Aitor himself, his hair blazing white in the infrared, asleep with his chin up.

Suddenly he jerked. Then his arms crossed in his lap. A moment later, his head moved left to right. His legs uncrossed, and he shifted at the hips.

Alice looked at the clock. 2.58. 'After the other two,' she said.

'Yes.'

'No bilocation – *tri-location* – or third ghost here, then.'

'No. I suspect it was one of the first two come down to see me.'

'This isn't making any sense to me. At all.'

'No. Me neither. But there's a little something nudging its way out of a corner of the Aitor mind. I can feel it.'

'Good. While it does that, I've more to tell you, too,' said Alice. 'Something very strange happened to me yesterday as I was coming back from the beach.' She proceeded to tell him the story about the quadbiker, Andrew Knight.

'Did you get his details?' said Aitor, when she finished.

'Yes,' said Alice. 'I filmed him giving them to me.'

'Let me see.'

'My phone's in my room. I'll forward it to you.'

'Good. That sounds suspicious to me. He was in the woods, you say? Just here?'

'Yes.'

'Near the old hospital?'

'Ye-es,' said Alice, thinking. Then she said: 'Which brings me to another thing. I spoke to one of the guests at breakfast this morning. Jo, he's a climbing centre manager from one of the Valleys. He turned out to be an amateur historian and he knew about the smallpox hospital. And – here's the thing – this house was part of it.'

'No!'

She nodded again. 'That makes it more likely that the ghost *is* that doctor, doesn't it? The suicide. Perhaps he hanged himself in this building.'

'Certainly seems possible,' said Aitor.

'So what do we do next?'

'There's too much,' said Aitor, blowing out his cheeks. 'You take it easy. You're on holiday after all. I can see you need to relax after seeing that video. We've done our surveillance, now it's back to the research part. I'm going to look through the online archives at Swansea University. That's where I found out about the man, the doctor. I want to see if I can find out anything more about him.'

53.

When Alice came downstairs she found a short woman
with a brunette bob in the hallway, holding the hand of
a little girl. She was still disturbed by the film, trying to
pin down a dozen fleeting ideas, and worried for a
moment about having to change tack and talk to a
complete stranger. But as she hesitated the woman
spoke, in a gentle Welsh accent.

'Hi. You must be Susannah's friend?'

'Yes, Alice.'

'I'm Bronwen. And this here is Katy. We've come for
a playdate with your boyfriend, haven't we Katy?'

'He's not my boyfriend!' exclaimed the girl. 'He's too
little.' She giggled. She was older than Jacob, maybe five
or six, and Alice had to admit she was exceedingly
captivating, with chestnut pigtails and a lot of freckles.

'Would you like to come too?' said Susannah,
emerging from the kitchen with Jacob in her arms. 'We're
going to Caswell Bay for ice cream.'

'Umm…' said Alice.

'Go on,' said Bronwen. 'You can have one too!'

'Well – OK,' said Alice.

54.

At Caswell beach Bronwen found three other mums with
their children so it turned into a far more lively – or
chaotic – event than Alice had anticipated.

Katy, pretty little girl that she was, turned out to be
intensely bossy and soon made cry the two children who

were helping her bury Jacob in the sand. Alice, who had been trying to help, watched helplessly as one, a little boy called Ricky with a heavy brow and hardly any chin, struck the second burier on the cheek with his spade. She tried to tell him to stop and thankfully Bronwen intervened, catching his arm just as he was about to land a second, much more vicious, blow. Alice sidled off to help another mum buy the ice creams.

The weather had been turning throughout the day and it was now mostly overcast. A breeze was coming in up the channel. The temperature had dropped a few degrees.

'More like your typical British summer,' said the mum, whose name was Theresa. She took a lick of her blackcurrant ice cream. 'They say it's going to rain later.'

'Couldn't last,' said Alice, smiling.

'You got kids of your own?'

'No.' Alice thought it was a strange question. If she did surely they would be here with her now?

'You've got plenty of time ahead of you for that. You a career woman?'

'I suppose so,' said Alice.

'What do you do?'

'I help run old heritage properties for visitors.'

'Oh, that sounds interesting,' said the woman.

They carried the cones back down the beach to the rest of the group. The children had given up burying Jacob and were starting to mark out a game of hopscotch in the sand. Katy was once again in the lead, instructing children smaller than herself what to do.

'Be nice, now, Katy,' said her mum, accepting two ice creams off Alice and handing one to her daughter.

Katy took the ice cream and licked it. The sun broke back through the clouds for a moment, lighting her up as she stood still on the damp sand. Then she lifted a finger and pointed at Susannah.

'Who is he?' she said.

Her mum looked over her shoulder. 'You know who that is, sweetness. That's Susannah, Jacob's mummy.'

Katy seemed to think for a moment, the cone tipping precariously in her hand.

'No,' she said. 'Not her – him!'

Bronwen looked at Susannah, who came closer to them.

'He's horrible,' said Katy. 'He is making me sick!' She hurled the uneaten ice cream across the sand. It hit Ricky's arm and splodged, top-down, on the sand.

Susannah looked behind her. 'There's – there's no one there,' she said, uncertainly.

'Look at his eyes!' screamed the little girl, and suddenly all the children became excited.

'Who?' shouted one.

'I see him,' screamed another little girl, spinning around, clearly not focusing on anything.

Jacob bounced up and down. 'You!' he shouted, pointing at Alice. 'You!'

Alice exchanged a concerned glance with Susannah.

'Has he ever been seen away from the house?' she said quietly.

'No, not as far as I know,' said Susannah.

With a final shout of 'You!', Jacob turned and began to run away across the sand, towards the sea. Susannah chased after him. And there, briefly, for one moment, Alice did see him, flowing behind her old friend – the man in the suit. And then he was gone, evaporated with the sea breeze.

'She's looking at me – stop her!' said Ricky.

His mum, a woman with long, frizzy hair and wearing a brown jumper, looked at Alice. 'She's not, Ricky,' she said.

'Not her – her!'

Alice looked at the boy, he was looking straight at her, not off to her left or right. She felt a strangeness creeping over her, the situation taking on a heightened, surreal energy as the parents tried to control their increasingly alarmed children.

She looked up at the sky, grey-clouded now, and saw a kite with a green tail fluttering overhead. The children were shouting around her. Susannah was coming back with a wailing Jacob thrashing in her arms. He wanted to go to the sea. Bronwen was saying in an increasingly loud voice that it was time to go home. Katy was shaking her head and complaining, why should they have to go just because *he* had turned up, and besides, her ice cream was ruined and she wanted another one. Ricky and the small girl who had been burying Jacob were holding hands and jabbering and licking their ice creams as the wind picked up from the sea.

Alice's head swam. She wanted to scream. She wanted to escape.

What was happening to her?

55

Back in the Mercedes, Susannah handed Jacob her phone in the child seat to keep him quiet. He'd kept up a non-stop mix of talk and babble since the collective hysteria on the beach.

'You need to see Aitor's videos when we get back,' said Alice. 'Something extremely weird is going on here.'

Susannah nodded, glancing at the rear-view mirror as she started the engine. 'Don't I just know it,' she said.

'There were three recordings that indicated visitations last night,' Alice continued. 'You, me and Aitor, asleep on the couch, all received one. But the freaky thing is, yours and mine happened at exactly the same time.'

'Huh?' said Susannah. 'What does that mean?'

'Aitor's best guess is that there are two.'

'What! Two ghosts? No way. One's already ruining us…'

'I spoke to Jo, too, this morning. Did you know Peacehaven was a part of the smallpox hospital?'

'It's a separate building. A few hundred metres away. How could it be?'

'It was a potential overflow facility,' said Alice. 'But because there weren't many cases, they only used it for admin and storage.'

'Do you think the doctor hung himself in *our* house?'

'Maybe. Aitor is seeing if he can find anything else about it online.'

'I need a cigarette,' Susannah muttered.

Alice felt a surge of sympathy. 'Look, I know now how much you and Gareth have been through. I can see what it's doing to you. But I'm going to help you through it.'

'But what are you going to do?' Susannah tugged anxiously at her hair. 'How can you or this Spanish guy help? I don't see what any of us can do. Sometimes, I feel like I may as well…'

'Susannah!' said Alice.

'Give up,' said Susannah. 'I was going to say give up.'

'We need to try and corner him,' said Alice. 'If I can get into the same space as him, perhaps I can find out why he's here. And then perhaps I'll be able to help him to get where he needs to be.'

Susannah looked doubtful, then laughed grimly. 'It all sounds like so much hokum. Wishful thinking. Let's say it is this doctor, and he's hanging – sorry, poor term – *staying* around because he couldn't cope with the grief of losing all those kids to smallpox. What are we supposed to do about that? I appreciate what you and Aitor have done, are doing, but what if, in the end, there's no solution? What if we're stuck with this ghost forever? What if he's following us? Because that's what Katy saw on the beach, surely? She must have seen him somewhere. She said he had horrible eyes, didn't she?'

Alice stared down at her lap.

'Perhaps – in the worst-case scenario – have you thought about moving? Going back to Cardiff or Surrey?'

'We can't,' said Susannah quietly. 'We don't have the money. Everything we had was sunk into that house. And then there was all the subsidence costs. Our finances… they are such a mess. You wouldn't believe it. If only that Italian priest could have got us a bloody exorcist.'

56.

As they drew up the drive, Alice saw Aitor sitting on a small seat at the front of the house sipping from a small expresso cup. His head turned when he heard the car.

Whilst Susannah took Jacob into the kitchen for his tea, Alice went and sat down beside Aitor. She told him about the episode on the beach, the confusion and chaos of the children.

'Alice, I don't know what's going on here,' he said. 'You see ghosts. And Susannah, you told me she saw the ghost – the one of Charlotte's grandmother – when you were children. But you only caught a brief glimpse of him on the beach – and Susannah saw nothing.'

'Yes.'

'It doesn't make sense,' he said. 'Even less so, when I tell you what I've found out this afternoon.'

'Oh?'

'I told you I was searching the University archive? Well, I didn't find anything there. But then I took out a sub to the British Newspaper Archive and managed to find a local paper from the time of the epidemic. It had a story about the doctor. The title is something about *The Doctor who died of a Broken Heart*. I'll show it to you when we go indoors. But – here's the thing – there's a detail in it that throws everything we've thought into doubt.'

'What?'

'It says that he hung himself by jumping from the hospital mezzanine.'

'Gruesome.'

'Yes – and one, that means he didn't hang himself in this building.'

'But he could still roam, couldn't he? I've seen the Farthingbridge girl in the Summer House, the pantry, in the woods above the lake, and outside in the forecourt. And Charlotte's grandmother…'

'Yes, darling. I don't contest that they can roam. But I still think they are *most likely* to haunt one place, the place they died, or where their biggest grievance lies.'

'I think that would include here,' said Alice. 'It was part of the hospital. And if they need the living, as they seem to, this is the place he would most likely come. As the other place is pulled down.'

'OK, that was point one,' said Aitor. 'I don't disagree with you. But there was something else that occurred to me when I read the article. I did some further search about hanging afterwards. Several ghost sightings – the more credible ones – have involved hangings. But only in a couple of cases did they appear with the horrible, distorted features of this Peacehaven man.

'When the government used to hang people, they were all dropped suddenly, normally by a trap door opening beneath their feet. They called this the Long Drop, or Measured Drop, making sure that the rope was the exact right length for the height and weight of the prisoner to ensure a speedy death – by a broken neck.'

'More gruesome.'

'But from everything you said about this ghost, his bulging eyes, green tongue, swollen face – these are different effects from those of the Long Drop. Those symptoms are caused when the suicide asphyxiates themselves, usually from a low point of suspension – say a door handle or bed post – using their body weight to exert the pressure.'

Alice wrinkled her nose.

'The suffocation is gradual and results in a build-up of fluid in the face that's been forced out of the veins, with the blueness caused by deoxygenated blood.'

'Are you trying to make me chuck?' said Alice.

'Stay with the science,' said Aitor. 'It's a favourite method for prisoners to kill themselves, when there's no hook or other high point they can drop themselves from. But it's also used in a lot of domestic circumstances.'

'Isn't it possible that happened to the doctor?' said Alice. 'Maybe he jumped but for some reason his neck didn't break and he suffocated slowly, suspended in mid-air. Or perhaps…' she shuddered to think of it, '…perhaps he fell and caught the rope and was hanging on to it trying to stop the pressure? Maybe he regretted it as soon as he did it? That's something I've heard is common with suicides.'

'Possible,' said Aitor. 'But unlikely. Very unlikely in my opinion. And something else that's been troubling me,' he added. 'If he was a good man, a doctor, why would he be haunting a guest house? That woman who saw him was lucky to survive her fall down the stairs.'

'Maybe that was just an accident. He might be trying to communicate something we're all failing to understand.'

'You're right,' said Aitor with a wry smile. 'It can't be easy, being a ghost.'

'My head aches.'

'Mine too.'

Alice took a deep breath. 'I suppose I'd better go tell Susannah.'

'Hold on, will you?'

'Why?'

Aitor paused, considering. 'I'm starting to have a hunch about something I found earlier. Especially after this incident you just described, about what happened with the kiddies on the beach. I think it's probably better that – well, maybe that she continues not to rule out the doctor for a while. I don't know, it's all half-formed.'

'Tell me,' said Alice. 'Even if it is just half-formed.' She hated people being cryptic.

'Bear with me,' said Aitor. 'I've heard that some writers – and detectives – don't like to divulge their crazy ideas before they've had a chance to properly formulate and explore them themselves. Sometimes the ideas can be killed by bringing them out too soon into the light of day. They need to brew in the darkness of the mind. I'm a bit like that.' His eyes twinkled at her.

Alice shook her head, in mock disbelief.

'Later, darling.' He smiled. 'Aitor promises.'

'Not much later,' she said. 'This place is starting to really mess with my head.'

His cow-brown eyes looked at her with concern. 'Not triggering past traumas, I hope?'

'Everything triggers past traumas for me,' she said, rolling her eyes.

'You were going to show me the video of the man. The one with the quadbike.'

'Oh yes – here.' She dug the phone out of her pocket, opened up the app. 'Here.'

Aitor watched the video of Andrew Knight giving his details to Alice in the wood.

After a while she became aware of an atmosphere in the air, an increase in his level of concentration. He held the phone closer to his face.

'What? What is it?'

155

'Let's go and have a look at this on my laptop,' he said. 'I want to see it in more detail.'

57

'Look – there – there!'

Alice peered closely at the screen. 'Nope. I see nothing.'

Andrew Knight was detailing his phone address when Aitor froze the frame.

'In the back there, just over his right shoulder. There's a kind of misty line on the tree.'

Alice squinted.

'Compare it to the other side. The pine branch there is clear – your camera's good, its definition is very good...'

'Thank you.'

'But on this side, see how there is more fuzz. And – let me move the image forward a few frames – see! See how it appears to be moving, whilst keeping in his shadow.'

'It's possible, I suppose,' said Alice. 'But isn't it just the sunlight?'

'I don't think so.'

'Then what do you think it is?'

'Normally you can't see spirits on ordinary cameras,' said Aitor. 'But there are instances when it's happened. There was a famous one on one of the first daguerreotypes, a picture of a ghostly girl in the background of a print. That *was* a fraud – just a previous print that hadn't been properly cleaned from the frame – but there have been others since that have much more credibility. They're few and far between, which is why I don't really hope to capture them that way myself, why I've created my camera/EMF/timer combo. But this – I think this one might be a ghost.'

'Behind the man?'

'Possibly. *Possibly*.'

'What then, Aitor?'

'Not behind. In the man?'

58.

Alice thought for a moment.

'You mean – he was possessed?' she said.

Aitor raised his eyebrows, blew out his cheeks. 'Possibly.'

'That – that might make sense,' said Alice. 'He stopped abruptly when I screamed at him. Then he was confused when I questioned him, almost as if he wasn't himself.'

'You made him jump right out of his skin,' said Aitor, raising his eyebrows. 'Or perhaps *the ghost* jump right out of his skin.'

'It was near the hospital ruins,' said Alice.

'The plot thickens.'

'Just as we thought it was thinning.'

They both chuckled.

'I can't believe we're actually laughing,' said Alice.

'Sometimes it's the only way, darling.'

She sat back, staring out of the window. 'So all you've managed to do today is confuse me, Aitor. Confuse me *more*. It looks like the doctor isn't our ghost. Does that make the hospital irrelevant or not? Maybe not, if the quadbiker was somehow possessed whilst in its proximity. But why would someone – anyone? – want to kill or scare me like that? And now there's not one ghost but two to identify. Both of which are plaguing us in the middle of the night. Like vampires. Which might, come to think of it, explain why I have this bloody awful pain in my neck all the time.' She reached up and squeezed the muscles between her shoulders and neck.

'All good questions,' said Aitor. 'Give me time.'

She looked at him.

'How about we stay up tonight?' she said.

'You thought I was going to bed?'

'No,' she said, smiling. 'But what if I stay up with you and we live-watch the cameras?'

'On a rotational basis.'

'Yes, one at a time is better than nothing,' said Alice. 'Then if we see one of the cameras go on, I can go to it. If the man in the brown suit is there, I can try and do my *thing*.'

'Your ghost-meld.'

'Yes.'

Aitor nodded slowly. 'It sounds like a fantastic plan, darling.'

59.

'You look exhausted. Can I make you coffee?'

Alice found Susannah in the kitchen, slumped in an easy chair in the corner, staring up at the ceiling. There was a packet of cigarettes on the table beside her and Alice could smell a staleness in the air. She guessed

Susannah had just been out for a fag on the terrace, after putting Jacob to bed.

'I am. And yes please.'

Alice put the kettle on and spooned some coffee into the cafetiere. She didn't say anything, sensing Susannah's need to unwind. Having a small child was hard. Running a business was hard. Worrying about money was hard. And then, on top of all that, being haunted by a ghost… She poured the hot water into the glass jug and felt her old antipathy towards her friend draining away. After all, even if she was suffering, Susannah had jumped far more of life's hurdles than her. Alice had no husband or children and, whilst she loved her job, it didn't have anywhere near the same level of challenge and responsibility as running your own business. It was as if Susannah had walked a high wire, with no safety net – and she, Alice, was trudging along down on the ground.

No, all her life had been was a reaction to one random trauma after another – with a whole lot of paranormal activity thrown in for good measure. But, she supposed, at least she had got through those knocks – or to be more accurate, body blows. She didn't think she was being overly arrogant to think most people couldn't have handled something like Bramley pretty much entirely on their own.

These conflicting thoughts flitted through her mind as she poured the coffee and took it over to the woman in the corner. She pulled a chair away from the dinner table and sat down beside her.

'Nice and strong,' said Susannah, sipping the cup. 'That'll bring me back to life.'

Alice had heard that bags under the eyes were not really a sign of tiredness, but she couldn't believe it in this instance. Susannah's were dark grey, her whole face ashen. 'Is there anything I can do for you?' she said. 'You're carrying a lot here.'

Susannah stared at her. For a moment, Alice felt the shadow of shyness and looked down, but then lifted her head and met Susannah's gaze. She remembered how much she had admired the startling, grey-flecked green of her eyes. They were still as beautiful, more so tinged with the sadness of life.

'You always were a good girl, Alice,' said Susannah. 'Sorry, that sounds patronising, I didn't mean it like that. You always were a good person. I'm sorry that things went so wrong between us at school. That *I* went wrong between us. Can you imagine how our lives might have been if we'd stayed friends?'

Alice had never considered that. But, doing it now, she realised she had never had another friend like Susannah. Charlotte had been a good companion, but they hadn't shared their hopes, hadn't talked about books and art and films and dreams, in the way that she and Susannah had. And then, after Charlotte, she'd had a few friends at college and one or two through work. But never strong like that. Nothing potent, heady.

'Perhaps quite different,' was all she managed to say. She could feel emotions stirring, coming up like an undertow from the seabed. Hope and fear and joy and love and something encompassing them all…

Sadness. She wanted to cry. How embarrassing.

'I never had another friend like you,' said Susannah, as if reading her mind.

'Me neither,' she said.

'The unfathomable workings of the human heart.'

Alice nodded. She felt glassy-eyed, worried that if she said something she really might blub.

'Alice. I really am sorry. For – everything.'

'Yes, I know,' said Alice. 'Thank you.' She wiped the corner of her eye with her sleeve. When she looked up she thought Susannah seemed on the verge of tears too.

'You're setting me off,' said the blonde woman.

'Tired and emotional,' said Alice, smiling.

'Hardly surprising, with everything we've been through.'

'You're right. We've both done well to survive.' Suddenly, Alice had a moment of giddy joy. She might not have a family, adult responsibilities – but she was free.

'We are both doing well,' said Susannah.

The moment of buoyancy passed. Alice sniffed, straightened her back. 'I'm going to find him, Susannah,' she said. 'With Aitor's help, I'm going to find him – tonight. I'm going to find out what he wants. And, if I can, I'm going to help him cross over.'

Susannah's eyes shone. 'Thank you, my friend,' she said, quietly.

Alice gazed at her. What was that look on the woman's face? Apprehension? Anxiety? She really couldn't tell.

60.

They finished dinner early that night, eating indoors because of the cooler weather and rain showers.

Susannah was yawning repeatedly and headed up to bed shortly after nine. Alice wished that she could go too, she was shattered, but she knew she must stay up with Aitor. The Basque went to his room and brought down his laptop and his bag of ghost hunting paraphernalia, whilst Alice tidied the meal away and set the dishwasher going.

Aitor put the computer on the kitchen table and tested the cameras. They closed the French doors and sat beneath the soft light of the brown globe that hung above the table.

'Your room... top floor landing... first floor landing... Jacob... sitting room,' said Aitor. 'We'll give Susannah a while to get into bed,' he added, winking at Alice.

Without the infrared beam activated, each room was black, displaying only its camera's number.

'I guess we can't see the EMF readings?' said Alice.

'Yes we can,' said Aitor. 'I've connected them with Bluetooth to my phone. But... this is the downer. They won't come on unless one of the cameras comes on.'

'So we need a person to move to trigger the EMF too.'

Aitor nodded. 'I'm planning to do some walkabout tours of the landings and lounge throughout the night with this handheld one. I've also got a thermometer that can check for cold spots.'

'I don't remember feeling any cold spots with ghosts before,' said Alice.

'No, I don't think they happen much, if at all,' said Aitor. 'But it's worth trying, lots of good people swear by them.'

'I'll do some tours too,' said Alice.

'OK. We can take it in turns.'

'Good.' She looked around the kitchen, at the double-height fridge, the prep island with its block of knives, the wooden playpen scattered with picture books, plastic vehicles, and soft toys. There was the swishing of the dishwasher, partially obscuring the low hum of the fridge. It all felt so… *ordinary*.

'So,' she said. 'What now?'

'We wait.'

61.

Aitor did a sweep of the building at 10.30. He showed Alice how to operate the EMF and the infrared thermometer, and she took her first tour at 11.30. When she came back downstairs, he was sitting in the easy chair, looking at his tablet.

'What you reading?' she asked, sitting down at the table.

'Just being nosy. Looking at our hosts on the net.'

'Naughty,' said Alice. Then, after a moment: 'Found anything interesting?'

'Mr Gareth Parry has had a long and distinguished career in the hotel industry, working in several European hotels as both Deputy and General Manager. Speaks French and Dutch. He was married to a French lady, but they got divorced before he came back to Cardiff. He had a child with her, but I'm guessing he doesn't see him.'

'You found out all this from the net?'

'Yes.'

'How?'

163

'Well, he doesn't have much of a social media presence,' said Aitor, touching his lower lip. 'But I found his wife, who was referred to by name in one of the old hotel website staff lists that hadn't been properly updated. It mentioned her profession too, a model, so I was able to find her on Facebook and Instagram. She does those kind of words-of-wisdom-type posts, and in one the comments from friends alluded to the divorce. And there were some photos of her son, a handsome boy into his reversed caps and Hip Hop.'

'You found all that out while I was doing my tour of the house?' said Alice incredulously.

'No,' he said. 'I've been looking on and off ever since you told me about the case,' he added, with a sheepish grin.

'Have you found out anything about Susannah?'

'She's a smart lady too. After getting an MSc in Management from Bristol University, she set up her first business as a cleaning company, supplying cleaners – mainly Polish cleaners – to homes in Winchester. There was a big gap in the market apparently. Then she moved into office cleaning with another, separate business – and from there into stationery with her third company.'

'I wouldn't know where to start with something like that,' said Alice. She realised how little she knew about the life of her friend – ex-friend, whatever she was now – in between school and now. 'What about her private life? Any other husbands?' She was a little ashamed of how eager she was to know.

'No, I'm still looking,' said Aitor, absent-mindedly, flicking through screens. He looked up. 'All I've found so far is a couple of business partners – the guy she mentioned from the stationery company and one from her first company. The cleaning company in Winchester.'

'A man or woman?'

'Another man – it's on Companies House.'

Monday – Last Day

62.

Alice woke with a start to a peculiar, wet sucking sound.

She looked up groggily from the kitchen table and saw that Aitor was tugging the fridge door open, surveying the contents. He reached into the bright interior and came away with a can of beer.

'I dozed off,' she said.

'Yes.' He smiled, cracking open the beer. 'Two hours ago.'

She ruffled her hair and looked at the blackness outside the French windows. 'What time is it?'

He peered at the laptop. 'Twenty past three.'

'Anything on the monitors?'

'No. It came on in Susannah's room for a minute or so, but I figured it was just normal movement in her sleep. No signs of anxiety.'

'Have you done another tour?'

'Two.'

Alice yawned. 'Guess it must be my turn, then.' She got up and poured herself a glass of water at the sink. She drank several big gulps down, then picked up the EMF and the infrared thermometer.

'Phasers on stun,' she said, lifting the thermometer at Aitor.

'Aye, aye, Captain.'

'See you in a little while.' She wandered out into the hallway, gloomily lit by every other of the wall-mounted shades.

Alice went into the sitting room – now dark, with just a rectangle of pale light from the doorway – and scanned the air with the readers. Nothing. She did feel how cold it was though, and shivered. There was some noise of wind outside the bay windows, and a faint rattle suggested rain.

She turned and headed back down the hall, checking the utility room, a small study that Susannah and Gareth used as their office, the formal dining room for guests with its unlaid round tables, and then a room filled with toys that was a playroom for Jacob. Each room she swept with the silent tools, watching the bright blue screen of the EMF and the red LED of the thermometer. Besides the occasional blip where the numbers fidgeted from zero to one or two, there were no significant changes to the volts per meter. And there were only marginal changes to the background temperature.

She retraced her steps to the entrance hall, then veered right up the wide stairway to the first floor, passing black-and-white pictures of Welsh screen idols, Ivor Novello, Jonathan Pryce, Catherine Zeta Jones and Anthony Hopkins amongst them. When she came up on to the landing and lifted the infrared thermometer it showed a drop in temperature, just ahead of her.

She looked around at the empty corridor. To the right it ran down to Jo's room and another guest room, ending in a window that faced the dark woods. Turning left, she walked past Jacob's room and another guest room, the one that had been occupied by the young men who'd left. This was where she'd been when she saw the hanged man the day before, and the temperature was now showing nearly two degrees cooler than the stairs. She crept forward, feeling the floorboards beneath the red carpet give a little with each of her steps, the creaking muffled by the thickness of the pile.

She passed another bedroom and the bathroom, carefully scanning each doorway, pushing the door a little to peek into the bathroom, feeling as if she was somehow looking with twice as much intensity as normal. She passed Susannah's room, noticing again the tension in her shoulders. She stopped, took a deep breath. Then spun round, thinking that there might be somebody behind her.

She stared back at the dimly lit, silent corridor.

Shaking her head, she carried on to the end of the landing and reached the stairs up to the top floor, her floor. The stairs were darker than the rest of the corridor.

She began to climb them.

63.

The tension in her neck was getting unbearable as she came up on to the second floor. She looked around at the open area with its small chair and table, on which a couple of lifestyle magazines had been neatly positioned. Beside the chair was a tall standing lamp, the only light on in the long corridor. In the sloping roof above her was the uncovered skylight, black, the murmur of wind and rain muffled by the double glazing.

She was definitely going to have to make an appointment to see an osteopath if her neck and back carried on like this. Aitor was probably right, it could be a pulled muscle that they hadn't picked up at the hospital and which hadn't been allowed to heal properly. Which was hardly surprising, given all the stress of Susannah and this place.

Moving on, Alice checked the bathroom, then headed down towards her own bedroom, the Reading room. She popped the thermometer into her jeans pocket to free a hand so she could grasp the door handle.

She frowned. Something wasn't right. The pain in her neck was becoming fierce, at first stinging, like the pain from nettles, and then sharp and jagged, like glass splinters. She let go of the handle and turned to look back from where she'd come.

'Shit!' she shouted.

The man in the suit was there, moving towards her fast, his arms flailing.

'What the…'

She backed into the doorway. He was coming right at her, the light behind him so that his swollen face, the wild eyes, were in shade.

But still she could see them, lit palely from within.

In her inner ear she thought she could hear a groan, the ghost groaning, wailing – or was it the wind? His body was twisting, only a few feet away from her now, she was going to shout again, cry out for Aitor but then she remembered what she had to do, she had to *go forward and meet him.*

But his arms, his large hands, they were grasping for her, violent, it felt violent, like he wanted to attack her, to strangle her, kill her…

'Brave, brave!' she hissed to herself.

And leapt forward at the grotesque ghost-corpse of the hanged man.

64

But as she jumped something unexpected happened.

The ghost dodged effortlessly towards the near wall and she missed him. She twisted to where he was now standing beside her, intending again to thrust herself into him. But as she moved she saw his eyes right before her own and gasped with the horror.

They bulged from their sockets, threaded with the darkness of swollen blood vessels. The eyelids and the ridge of skin below were thick and rubbery. The pupils were wide, black and fizzing with terror.

Then the hanged man's eyes swivelled away from hers and looked behind her, over her shoulder. She could see that his arm had risen again, slowly, pointing to something. Her throat dry, her skin shrinking against her skull, Alice turned her head to follow the gaze of the hanged man.

There was no one there. She was staring at a stylised painting of a large bird, edged in black, hanging on the wall.

Then she noticed something fuzzy, something in the darkness just below her eye level. Alice looked down.

And found herself staring at a girl, standing right behind her, in her shadow. A girl gazing up at her. A teenage girl with long, curled hair, close-set eyes, and a gash on her cheek. A girl wearing an old-fashioned, laced outfit.

The girl in the ivory dress.

Alice cried out in shock and stumbled backwards towards the man in the suit. And suddenly she was in a mist, a dreadful, pitiful mist, with the hint of ghostly arms stretching about her and…

65.

He has given all that he has. He can give no more.

His wife, his child, his money, his hope – everything. All gone. And now he is waiting, waiting for her one last time, to do the thing she has promised she will do.

To come.

He stares across the steering wheel out at the wan lights of the street on which he is parked. The angular, white bay windows of Edwardian terraces run away into the distance, like something Michael would make with his Lego. Rain drips. He waits.

She must come. She must, she said on the phone, this time, this time she would be here. She would come.

The rain intensifies on the windscreen, like a pouring of molten glass. His dreams melt with it.

He looks at the glove compartment, thinks about what he has in there, the drink and the tie.

Suddenly, he sees a shape in the gloom, walking down the pavement towards him, shielded by a large black umbrella.

This is it! It's her, he's sure of it. He feels his throat constrict, his passion bursting and drowning all at once. He's in a sweat, a cold sweat.

For a moment he imagines a different scenario, it's her but she has come with a whole new set of conditions. It will happen, it's still writ large in the stars, but first you must do this, and then that, and then the other…

How will he react if that happens? He looks again at the glove compartment. No, he will see, he needs her so badly, he must keep an open mind…

The umbrella is drawing closer now, he can see the rain bouncing off it in a silvery shimmer. For a moment he is surprised by his joy, imagining that old film, Singin' in the Rain. He could be so happy, he knows. If only this uncertainty would end. The agony.

He can see the legs now, it is a woman, in heels and stockings, a dark skirt, smart like her, her legs, hips, body increasingly visible as she approaches the car…

She is veering, stepping towards his door, but no, there's a broken paving slab with a puddle, she is stepping around it, and then she is there, right beside the door, he can see her face, her hair under the umbrella, her hair that's long too, but mousy brown, not blonde, and she doesn't glance at the car, she hasn't even seen him sitting there behind the wheel, doesn't even realise it's him because…

It's not her.

Something big grows inside him. It pushes out everything, his lungs, his heart, his mind. It feels like there's no room inside of him for him. Just this strange, surging, overpowering force.

Shall he wait? His eyes move to the clock, see the numbers. They are already wrong. The numbers are all wrong.

With a glance at the glove compartment, he starts the car, indicates, and pulls out neatly from between the other parked cars.

He drives away, in the rain.

66.

'Alice?'

She looked up through tears to see Aitor leaning down over her. She was sitting against the wall, opposite the picture of the bird. And she was crying.

'What happened?' he said urgently, sitting down beside her and putting an arm around her shoulder. She moved her head slowly from side to side.

'I saw…'

172

But she couldn't speak, the tears streamed and then sobs began to break out of her, from the bottom of her lungs, so she thought she wouldn't be able to breathe…

Aitor pulled her harder into his shoulder, twisting his own back awkwardly to give her an easier position on which to push her wet face.

'Aitor…' she gasped.

'All right,' he said. 'You'd been gone so long I came up after you, then I heard you cry out. You're all right, you're safe.'

'It was terrible,' she said.

'What? What happened?'

'Him… I was *in* him… It was just so awful… so sad…'

'Come on,' he said quietly. 'Come downstairs.'

She allowed him to lift her chin from his damp shoulder, to help her to her feet. Then he led her carefully back down through the house, to the warmth and light of the kitchen.

67.

Aitor offered her some brandy he found but she preferred tea with plenty of sugar. Once she had her hands wrapped around the hot mug she began to talk.

'He was there, just as I was about to check my bedroom. He came at me down the landing, I was scared for a moment because he was making all these wild gestures with his arms and hands.'

'How?' said Aitor, sitting beside her with another beer.

She pulled back from the table and mimicked the hanged man's motions.

'It almost looks like he was gesturing at *something*,' he said.

Alice nodded, taking her tea again. 'He was. I know it now. He was pointing at the girl from Farthingbridge. The girl in the ivory dress.'

'What?' said Aitor, jolting back in surprise. 'What do you mean?'

'As he approached I tried to move into him, like I did with Mary. But he sidestepped me, again pointing. I realised then that he was pointing behind me. And when I turned, I saw her there. Standing right – *there* – behind me, like my shadow.'

Aitor raked his bleached hair. 'Oh my God, Alice,' he said.

'Exactly. That's what I thought. And then, when I stumbled back, I must have done what I initially intended – I moved into the hanged man.'

'And?'

Alice looked down at the table. 'It was terrible, Aitor. He was sitting in a car, in a rainy street, waiting for someone. A woman. A woman he was desperately in love with. But he was married, with a family. He'd given up everything for her, his home, family, money. He was waiting for her to come to him.'

'An illicit rendezvous?'

'Perhaps. But Aitor – he was at his wits' end. I've never felt such abject misery. He kept looking at the glove compartment of his car. There was drink and his tie in there, I knew what he was thinking.'

'And she didn't come?' said Aitor.

'No. She didn't come.'

'What did he do?'

'He drove away. But he drove away with this thing inside him. This dreadful, soul-crushing force.'

'Despair,' said Aitor.

'Yes, I guess that'll have to do. Despair.' Alice pressed her forehead into the palms of her hands.

Aitor sucked in air around his teeth. 'Well, at least we can rule out the doctor theory now,' he said at last.

'He was contemporary,' said Alice. 'The streetlights, his car – they were modern. The brown suit was confusing, it looked old-fashioned, but it wasn't.'

'And he was pointing at the girl, who was behind you?'

'Yes. How on earth did she get *there*?'

'OK,' said Aitor. 'I think I can tell you my theory now. Things are starting to make sense to me.'

'What is it? What's your theory?'

'It's – well, ghosts don't just haunt places.'

'What do you mean?'

'They haunt people too.'

68.

'What?'

'I always remember something you said when you were telling me the story of Mary Stevens,' said Aitor. 'When you wanted to reunite her ghost with her son. You said it happened because there was somehow a bond between the pair of you.'

'Me and her. Yes, that's what it felt like. Some kind of… what's the word? Like a… *metaphysical* bond.

Something happening on a different plane. Or something. That's nuts, isn't it?'

'No, not to me,' said Aitor. 'No weirder than anything in modern physics, with all its *action at a distance*. I've been thinking about it a lot. And I think it relates to what's happening here, in Peacehaven.'

'Huh?'

'So you have an exceptional ability, Alice, to read the – for want of a better word – *minds* of ghosts. To feel, fleetingly, what they have felt. To know what they have seen, what they've experienced. It's like the spiritualists, letting the deceased speak through them. But it's your own thing, it's different because *you* are actually *inside* the ghost, as opposed to them being inside you.'

'So kind of like…' Alice felt herself struggling with words, ideas. It was so late, she was utterly drained from her encounter with the ghost. *Ghosts*. 'Like possession, but…'

'Yes, exactly, like possession but the other way round. *You* possess the *ghost*.'

'Don't say that,' said Alice. 'It's too weird.'

'But it's what happened?' said Aitor. 'It's what happened with Mary – and it's what just happened with this man.'

'I suppose it is kind of what happened.' Alice sighed. 'But what's that got to do with being haunted?'

'I think when that connection is made, a bond is created between you. Most ghosts seem to have a small, arbitrary range from the place of their death, or from the place where they experienced their special grief or pain. But when a bond has been made with a living person, I think they can leave that place, attached to their host.'

'You're doing my head in,' said Alice. She drew in a deep breath, gazed up at the globe lampshade. 'So let me get this straight. Just supposing you're right, then you're saying that Eloise, the girl from Farthingbridge, has… attached herself to me?'

'Yes. I think that's how she got here.'

'No…' began Alice, before suddenly sitting bolt upright on the chair. 'But yes – that would explain those children on the seafront pointing at the bus – and Jacob and the kids on the beach all pointing at me. Even the ghosts – the burning man, the hanged man – they both pointed at me. Well, not at me. At *her*. They've all been seeing her!'

Aitor's eyes were bright, swimming with a strange joy. 'Yes, I think so,' he said.

'She came with me from Farthingbridge to here… But why?'

'I don't know.'

Alice thought about the glimpse she'd had in the Summer House of the girl's soul, that deep, atrocious terror. 'Maybe there was someone – or *something* – in Farthingbridge that she wanted to get away from?'

'Quite possibly,' said Aitor, nodding.

'Wait! What about the burning man? Could it be him? Perhaps he was one of her tormentors alongside Ashford!'

'Possibly, who knows?' said Aitor. 'Or maybe the ghost of Ashford himself is there too.'

Alice shuddered. 'I just haven't seen him… And how come if she's…' she stopped. 'Oh my God! You mean – she's with me right now. She's in me – now?'

She spun round, looking behind her at the empty kitchen, half rising from her chair.

'Stay calm, darling,' said Aitor. 'Remember how you feel about ghosts, how they don't frighten you. And *you* have the power, it's in you.'

'This is freaking me out!' She could feel the tension in her shoulders and neck again, they had locked rigid. 'I'm imagining some kind of… *gremlin*, squatting on my back!'

It all made sense now, the headaches and stiffness she'd had for weeks. The strange mood swings, wanting to hit Susannah when she'd never hit a soul. No wonder she was feeling the strain, she was giving a kind of… *piggy-back* to a suffering ghost!

'All those dreams,' she said. 'That explains them. The terror of that girl – both of them, they were being chased by him, through the woods, by Ashford…'

'If she's here for protection, she's chosen you for your strength,' said Aitor.

'It still feels strange, just to know… God, she was there in the night – in my room, while I was sleeping!' She shuddered, thinking about the film, how she had sat up in bed and stared at the camera.

'Yes, probably,' said Aitor, his brown eyes moist with a mixture of excitement and concern.

'I want her off me!'

'Remember, Alice, she's a ghost. No ghosts are with us all the time. They are absent almost always, somewhere else entirely. Think of your planes analogy.'

Alice took a deep breath, collapsed back into the chair.

'This really is doing my head in,' she said. 'So many things at the moment – well all my life, really – they just do my head in.'

'You need sleep.'

'There's no way on earth I'm sleeping now. My mind is buzzing. As well as frazzled.' She was still shaking, it felt like the blood was shuddering through her veins.

Aitor was on his tablet beside her, flicking through search pages. Alice stared across the table, into space.

'I'm thinking so many thoughts,' she said. She glanced at the clock. 4:05.

'What about him – the hanged man?' she said. 'It was him who you were thinking of first, when you talked about people being haunted, wasn't it? Are you suggesting that it's not Peacehaven – it's *Susannah* who's being haunted?'

'You've seen him, haven't you?' said Aitor. He swung the tablet round to face her.

'Oh my God, it's him,' she whispered.

69.

He was handsome – beautiful, she might even have called him.

He had a long, pale face, with a fine nose, thin, almost colourless, lips, and a narrow chin. His hair was blond, wispy, retreating a little at the sides. His eyes, they did protrude a little, but you could see now they were blue, clear as the sky, almost ethereal, showing a kind, searching intelligence. He was almost unrecognisable from the creature she had seen the last two nights. Almost, but not quite.

It was him. The hanged man. That was for sure.

'Who is he?' she said.

Aitor flicked the screen and the picture shrunk to the top corner of a LinkedIn business profile.

'Dominic Turner,' he read. 'Company Director, Dancing Dusters.'

'Dancing Dusters? What the hell do they do?'

'Did. They were a cleaning agency, owned by two people. Dominic Turner – and Susannah Pugh.'

He flicked to a Companies House record, showing their names together as company owners.

'See where it's registered,' said Aitor.

Alice read the address: Clifton Road, Winchester.

'I told you that I was going through the British Newspaper Archives,' said Aitor, quickly tapping on to another open tab and bringing up an old news item from the *Hampshire Chronicle*. He spread his fingers across the tablet, enlarging the heading of a small article.

'Local businessman found dead,' Alice read aloud. She went quiet as she continued reading:

Dominic Turner, of Clifton Road, Winchester, was found dead in Winnall Moors Nature Reserve. Two teenagers discovered his body on the night of 15th April. The police are not treating the death as suspicious. His family have been informed.

'And this one,' said Aitor.

Local Businessman's Death was Suicide, Coroner's Report

Dominic Turner, of Clifton Road, Winchester, killed himself by hanging, the County Coroner reported to an Inquest on 30th April. Mr Turner ran a successful cleaning company, Dancing Dusters, with his business partner, Ms Susannah Pugh of Sparsholt. He is survived by his wife Patricia and their seven-year-old son.

'And just one more that came up with a search for him,' said Aitor.

Widow contests 'unethical' business arrangements of late husband

Patricia Turner of Clifton Road, Winchester, has appeared in the County Court contesting a Partnership Agreement between her late husband Dominic and his business partner, Susannah Pugh. Mr Turner and Ms Pugh were joint owners of successful cleaning firm, Dancing Dusters. The company had originally been set up with a 50-50 division of profits, but seven months before his death by suicide Mr Turner instructed his solicitor, Emma Jones LLB, to make changes to the agreement giving an 80-20 split to Ms Pugh. Mrs Turner contested the agreement on the basis of her husband being under undue influence from Ms Pugh, with whom he had been having an affair for some time. Despite allowing that the behaviour of Mr Turner had been 'depressing and immoral', Judge David Hargreaves ruled that there was no coercion and therefore rejected the claim. Mrs Turner stated outside the court that she intends to appeal the decision.

'I'm feeling sick,' said Alice. 'I'm guessing the appeal was unsuccessful?'

'I don't know,' said Aitor. 'I haven't found anything about it. But from the balance sheet of the first-year accounts of her next company, Winchester Office Cleaners, I'm guessing it was.'

'I suppose it doesn't matter either way,' said Alice, grimly. 'He's here to make her pay for what she did to him.'

'What he let her do to him,' Aitor corrected.

'Exactly,' said Alice, grimacing.

There was silence for a moment as they both thought.

'Shit,' said Aitor.

'What are we going to do?' said Alice. She felt suddenly weak with exhaustion, on the verge of collapse.

'Go to bed,' said Aitor. 'We'll work it out after we've had some sleep.'

'What about the ghosts?'

'What about them? What can they do?'

'Disturb our sleep,' said Alice, thinking again of her dreams, her strange performance in front of the night camera.

'Let them,' said Aitor.

70.

'See you in a couple of hours,' said Alice.

'Are you sure you don't want me to stay on your floor?' said Aitor.

She nodded. 'You need your sleep too. And I'll be all right.'

He grasped her shoulder briefly. 'If there's any more problems, you know where I am,' he said, then turned and headed back down the first-floor landing to his room.

With some trepidation, Alice began to mount the stairs towards her room. Step by slow step. Her shoulders ached and her head felt like it was soldered to her neck. She was deeply ill at ease with the idea of a ghost mysteriously bonded to her – no matter what that ghost might be running away from. For a moment she imagined herself as some kind of vehicle, an armoured car to get the girl to safety. Then a horrible image flashed through her head, of a wildlife programme about

Greenland sharks, lumpish, ancient creatures swimming through the cold sea with worm-like parasites eating away at their eyes. She didn't want something uninvited hitching a ride on her! What did she owe the dead?

She realised she was going to have to get back to Farthingbridge, to get into the building and somehow find the source of the girl's terror, so vividly experienced in her dreams. She couldn't go on like this. She shuddered, remembering all she knew about Lord Ashford and his parties. Whatever Eloise had experienced, it was certain to be detestable. But what could she, Alice, do to help her? Her tormentor had been dead for over two hundred years. Alice shook her shoulders, as if she might somehow shake her off.

How do you dislodge something that isn't really there?

It was all too much. And then, on top of that, there was Susannah. She felt a sudden, keen pain, like a slice from a knife. She remembered the moment earlier when, once again, for the first time in years, she had felt that rekindling of friendship. A deep connection. Her heart, guarded as it was through all these troubled years, had finally moved out into the open.

Only to find this.

Susannah had not turned a corner. She had not recovered something of the person Alice had thought she was. In fact, Alice now wondered whether that person had ever even existed, or whether she had just been a figment of her imagination.

A squalid affair. Cheating a wife and child out of their inheritance. How could she do that? Whilst Dominic Turner sure as hell carried the bulk of the blame, there was no way Susannah was squeaky clean. Alice knew how she operated. *The cow.*

Some people just don't change, she thought, feeling a wild, momentary anger flare inside her. This time, she would not forgive her.

But now, as she saw her bed, she realised she just needed to get her head down.

She was just so… bloody… tired…

******

71.

She becomes aware of the sound of snipping, right beside her ear.

Wait, that's too close, she thinks. *It's going to cut my ear.*

And then she realises. Someone is snipping scissors, just above her bed.

Her chest constricts, she wants to lurch away – but can't. She is stuck. There's a white cloud of fog around her. She hears the scissors snicking again, a hissing, looping sound, and fears for her ear. Someone is going to cut the edge of her ear soon. Someone wants to hurt her!

She is aswirl with panic, tries to push herself up on the sheets – but she can't for the life of her move. In fact, she can scarcely breath. What is wrong with her? She tries to scream, she can feel it in her ears, a pressure, but her jaw, her teeth remain clenched.

She cannot move. And the girl – how does she know that, even when she cannot see her? – is going to snip her ear off.

And then she realises. She is asleep. No, not asleep. In sleep paralysis. Awake, her mind alive, but unable to move, her muscles dead to the world. She has experienced this twice before in her life, once when she was a little girl and the second time as a student, the time that geeky boy doing English had plied her with those rotten brown magic mushrooms. She had enjoyed it at the time but the sleep paralysis incident that night – in which she saw her young, fresh-faced tutor expose himself in the corner of her room, and had panicked as she tried and failed to get up and flee – had put her off drugs for life.

So, she is awake now but cannot move. That means the girl is about to cut her ear and all she can do is fight against the inert lump of her foggy body.

Snip, snip, the scissors slice the air.

Her mind lurches like a prisoner bashing against the bars of her body – and then she realises…

72

It is her dress that she's cutting with the scissors.

Snip, snip, there go two more of those little pearly buttons, popping off on to the brown mulch of oak leaves on the ground. She stares at them for a moment, loving the mottling, the hint of yellow, the suggestion of magnificent clouds in miniature, which she can now see in the soft dawn light. A white rabbit, squatting awkwardly in the soil, sniffs at the buttons with twitchy nostrils.

'Not for you, *méchant lapin*,' she says, remembering how the rabbit had suddenly sprang out of her arms and she had to chase and catch it in the corner of the Summer House. 'You were a very naughty bunny, running away from me like that.' She lets the dress lie in her lap, the large scissors too, and looks back over her shoulder, through the trees and down across the lake towards the great neo-classical pile.

Farthingbridge.

She is planning to have so much fun there with her Barty, the second Lord Ashford. So much fun and mischief.

She turns back and, leaving the scissors in her lap, holds her ivory dress up in front of her. She giggles, seeing it sag at the waist with the big cut, like a stabbed lady. A lady of the court, sliced through her midriff. What a thought!

Quickly, she makes several more cuts in the dress then lifts the rabbit by its ears and, evading its desperate kicks, snips its white throat. She holds it down hard on her white dress, watches wide eyed as it shivers and jerks and bleeds away.

When the rabbit has stopped its shuddering and the dress given to her on her fifteenth birthday by her great-aunt Lina is suitably smothered in its blood, she lifts it away and carefully rubs the dress into the earthy forest mulch. A robin redbreast flicks over to check out what she's doing.

'Look at you standing there, with your little red cravat,' she says lightly, as she works.

Then she stands up, tosses the blood-stained rabbit into the brambles and heads deeper into the wood to find a place to stash her once-beautiful dress.

She is still carrying the scissors…

73.

…which she uses now, snip, snip, snip, to cut away the side of Alice's brain and there – there! – she steps nicely inside, and Alice realises that she can once again use her muscles, control her body.

Only it is not her now who is moving them.

It is the girl in the ivory dress.

74.

She, Eloise Bossuyt, is now mistress of the flesh, blood, bones and organs once occupied by Alice Deaton.

She sits up in bed, looks around at the still-dark room, at the faint grey light on the curtain. Looks up at the wardrobe, to the tiny red dot, the monitoring light of the camera perched on the top. She stares at it, smiling. Then she turns her legs to the side and climbs up off the bed.

She walks towards the far wall and the bookcase, holding her hands out in front of her, feeling for the place she knows the low shelf to be. Her fingers touch folded cotton, knock a small pot of needles, then bump up against something cool, hefty – metal.

She inserts her thumb and first three fingers into the bows of the dressmaker's shears.

Then she heads out of the door and down through the quiet, pre-dawn house, saying softly to herself:

'One for you, and one for me…'

75.

The thing is, she's still there, boxed in by the monstrous force of the girl's spirit, trapped in the tiniest, most remote corner of her own mind.

Alice is weak, as unfocused as the whole of the sea, but still she sees, she understands.

She understands all of it.

She understands how and why this girl became a monster. How from an early age her father would pinch her between the legs whenever she started crying, and how her mother would laugh instead of help. How before she had even reached puberty she was involved in lewd acts with family and friends at her father's notorious parties. How her trepidation and bewilderment had moved increasingly to perverse enjoyment in her early teens, an understanding of the Bossuyt *family way* of doing things. And of concealing those things once done. She began to take pride in it. Alice sees how Eloise had delighted in hating people, often openly alongside her mother and father, who would encourage her and fill her mind with the feebleness and worthlessness of humanity. Who ensured that she learned the manners of the court at all times, and appeared beyond reproach, despite the filth and depravity of the family behind the scenes. Who covered it all up when Eloise accidentally pulled a cord too tight around the neck of an elderly relative, at five o'clock one morning during a tumultuous party.

Her first murder.

Oh, how she had loved watching those rheumy old eyes as they gazed up at the chandelier with its gilded rosette, how they had rolled further to stare over the back of the settee, bulging, flicking left to right, then – oh, the perfection – stopping. Moving no more.

Alice sees how Eloise's aunt Camilla had brought her away to England when the rumours began to circulate about the death. There, as soon as she met her cousin, the young Lord Ashford, she had recognised in his careless red curls, his hooded eyes and thin lips, a kindred spirit. A weaker spirit, but a kindred one, nonetheless. Alice sees the heady experiences of their first weeks together, discovering each other's pleasures alongside those already ensconced in his house, under Ashford's wildly irresponsible patronage. The artists, gamblers, roués, thieves and… gentlemen.

But then there was the shock, when her mother insisted that she return to Bruges after the storm had died down. How could she take her away from this sublime existence, where every forbidden pleasure was within reach? For the first time in her life, Eloise plotted to deceive her own parents, working out a scheme with Bartholomew and his mother, who knew her son would not cope now without his petite Belgian paramour. She would cut up her own dress so that it would be assumed she had been abducted, killed. When all she did was go to London, buy new clothes, a dark wig, and adopt a beauty spot, then return to Farthingbridge as a new debutante, the supposed sister of one of the lesser-known hangers-on. And thus she had stayed in the house, enjoying a life of hedonism, a life heightened by the pain of (principally) others. The only challenge had been when her mother had sent one of her elderly friends to find her, which led to the trial, but they had weathered that one out, aided by the lack of evidence. Eloise had sojourned to Ashford's friend's house in London throughout the statesman's visit.

It was a life that, as she indulged it, as she systematically destroyed innocence, both hers and others', with her lover, Eloise realised she could never be without. And that had led her to the nefarious arts shown to her initially by her mother, the incantations and circle spells that would conjure dark forces, willingly offering her young soul up to whichever demon would take it in exchange for everlasting life.

Who knows whether those spells had any effect? Those spells that involved not only animal but also human sacrifices, including the girl, the servant girl, the one in the dream who Alice now realised had not been running *with* Eloise away from Ashford, but away from both of them.

Who knows what effect those incantations had?

All Eloise did know was that when she died, less than a year later, falling headfirst from the roof when she was drunk and dancing on a moonlit night…

She came back.

Back to haunt the living, to continue with her delight in caprice, destruction and evil.

A pursuit that she soon found enabled her to possess the living, to dominate the spirits of the inferior or the downtrodden or – as in Alice's case now – the sheer *exhausted*, and to do with them what she would. It was a power that had led her twice to burn down Farthingbridge, exulting in the fiery destruction. The first time was when the terminally boring, law-abiding fourth Lord Ashford had got so on her nerves that she had possessed his morphine-loving valet to torch his bed chamber one night – turning the Lord into the troubled ghost, the Burning Man.

And the second time, when she had come across her nemesis.

A woman who at first she had scarcely noticed, she appeared so plain and ordinary.

But who had one day seen her in the Summer House and, just as Eloise had been preparing to scare the wits out of her, had done that thing, that shocking, defiling invasion of her *space*. And in that moment Eloise had known the full story of Alice Deaton, of what she had done to ghosts in the past, how she had with her unique ability helped them to cross over, to be gone to the one place Eloise feared above all others, the place of no return.

She realised then, with absolute certainty, she would have to do all she could to destroy this woman.

Before Alice, in her soulless naiveté, destroyed her.

From an indescribable place inside her own soul, Alice sees it all.

She sees how Eloise seized Femi – poor, grieving Femi – and took her to that long-lost book of matches at the back of the fireplace, which she used to start the fire. How she had attempted to possess Alice when she was at her most distracted, cutting down the Caravaggio, and spat and cursed the fourth Lord Ashford, the Burning Man, as he tried to alert Alice to the ghost girl digging into her spine. How moments later she had separated from Alice to seize another opportunity, to possess Mike and shove the ladder.

And then how she had stayed within Alice's aura, unable to possess her, but still able to haunt her, shadow her, coming all the way here, to Peacehaven, being spotted by thoughtless children. How she had possessed that guileless young man on his quadbike to try and once again destroy the woman she feared would be her undoing. How Alice's sudden cry had brought him back to his senses, dispelling Eloise back into Alice's aura.

Alice sees it all with an abject horror, realising there is nothing she can do.

She is trapped in here, trapped alive, too enfeebled by exhaustion and stress to even attempt to take back control of herself.

78.

'One for you, one for me…'

She, the witch-girl, Eloise, says the words again as she comes down into the gloomy hall and crosses to the kitchen, the chunky scissors held loose in her fingers.

What does she mean by that? thinks Alice, panicking, unable to breathe, thumping against invisible walls.

The kitchen is dark, the lights switched off by Aitor when he left for bed, although there is just the faintest greyness from the pre-dawn. She moves over to the double oven, the DeLonghi with its chunky black grid of gas burners. She tugs three dish cloths out from where they are hung over the oven handle and lays them out beside the oven, along the counter. She picks up the large plastic bottle of vegetable oil and glugs it out, saturating the cloths.

Then she turns on the gas and jams her thumb on the electric ignition button.

No! Alice watches through eyes no longer hers alone as the ring and soon after the cloths ignite.

'One for you, one for me,' says the girl, with a voice that is not her own.

She turns and leaves the burning kitchen, still clutching the scissors.

79.

She walks back up the stairs, past the black-and-white movie idols, on to the first-floor landing.

Barefoot, she steps slowly along the plush carpet, passing the bedroom doors.

Not Jacob, thinks Alice, realising that this is what it must be like to be in hell. Saturated by atrocity, witnessing the most wretched evil, yet unable to act.

She passes Jacob's door, then the room where the young men had been staying.

'You're watching me, aren't you?' Eloise says to Alice in a loud voice. In *Alice's* voice. 'I can feel it.'

Alice tries to summon will, any power she has. To no avail. Hell. This is hell.

They come to Aitor's door and Alice screams against a mighty, invisible wind.

They walk past and arrive at Susannah's room.

And then, as her hand reaches down to grasp the brass door handle, Alice understands.

The *one for her* is the old friend who betrayed her. Who has betrayed her again with her deceit. But why bother killing Susannah? Alice wonders – before immediately realising.

For the joy of it. When it comes to murder, Eloise *is* actually counting, and each new kill is a badge of honour.

'Yes,' Eloise says softly as she turns the handle. 'We'll make sure she doesn't survive the blaze, just for you.'

80.

The room is dark, the only sound the quiet tick of a bedside clock.

But she knows the layout of the room, from when she helped Aitor set up the cameras and monitoring equipment. She looks up and sees the pinprick of red light on the dressing table, the light blinking now as the camera comes on, triggered by her moving towards the bed, lifting her arm, parting the heavy blades of the shears, stopping at the edge of the bed where she can vaguely make out the head of the woman, her hair splayed around her on the grey pillow like a gorgon.

She can hear her breathing softly, the ever-so-slight whistle of air in her nostrils.

Her arm rises to its full extent, preparing the heaviest blow.

And then, suddenly, there is brightness on the other side of the bed, a rushing shimmer of light coming at her and she stumbles back with a gasp of shock.

It is him. The man in the brown suit.

The hanged man.

81.

He comes at her fast and all she can see is the ferocious bulge of those eyes, burning into her soul with a perishing anger. It is as if he is roaring, yet there is no sound at all.

Startled, she stumbles back, her heel hitting something on the floor, a shoe perhaps, and she falls quickly backwards.

Her head hits something sharp, hard, and everything goes black.

******

Alice opened her eyes into bright, electric light.

For a moment she was completely bewildered, hearing noises, shouts, screams. Feeling a searing pain in her head. Seeing a white ceiling, with a small glass light in the centre. Smelling a familiar smell… burning. People were moving quickly around her.

Then it all returned. The girl, gas stove, scissors, Susannah, the hanged man flying at her.

And then she realised… she was back to herself, no longer possessed. Relief at being freed from the suffocating horror flooded through her.

Groggily, she propped herself up and tried to take in what was happening.

'Susannah – are you…'

Someone was speaking behind her, in a voice she knew, not well. The accent, Welsh, a man… Jo.

'No!'

It was Susannah who had screamed. Alice could see her, sitting up on her knees in bed, in her pyjamas. She was looking at the door. Alice turned, watched as the man stooped down to pick up something from the floor.

The scissors…

Alice looked up at Jo's weather-beaten face. Saw the peculiar focus in his eyes as he turned and advanced towards the bed, lifting up the scissors.

The Welshman was a light sleeper. He must have heard her talking again, as she moved down the corridor. Come to investigate.

And now… the girl in the ivory dress had possessed *him*.

One for you, one for me…

Alice knew what the girl meant. Susannah was for her, Alice, certainly; but the one for me – that had to be Alice herself. She was going to kill her after she had killed Susannah. She was a psychopath, pure and simple.

Her head reeling, Alice clambered to her feet. She watched as Susannah leapt off her bed towards the far wall, escaping a sudden slice of the scissors.

Where was the hanged man now?

Jo lurched across the bed, trying to grab Susannah as she screamed again and crashed into the curtains. Then Alice saw the ghost, Dominic, lunging at Jo.

But this time Eloise ignored it. Dominic's only power, the element of surprise, had gone. He vanished.

As Susannah narrowly avoided another lunge by Jo, backing up into the corner of the room, Alice realised she had to do something.

'Eloise – stop!' she shouted.

The possessed man turned.

He looked at her, a fit, middle-aged man with a broad jaw, a hangdog expression. Mouth slightly open, breathing heavily. The blades of the dressmaker's shears open at his side.

Susannah looked at her too, hand over her mouth.

Then Jo jumped on to the bed, heading for Alice, his eyes ablaze.

She turned and ran out of the room.

The pain in her head forgotten, Alice ran for her life.

She ran down the landing towards the stairs, screaming as she went. Behind her, she could hear banging, the pounding steps of the man as he chased her.

'Aitor!' she yelled, as she reached the top of the stairs. He would not be able to help her, but she had to wake him up, to give him a chance to save himself from the fire. She knew that Susannah would at least save Jacob.

'Come back, you bitch!' shouted Jo, only a few metres behind her.

She leapt down the stairs, several at once, bouncing her shoulder hard into the wall at the half-landing, turning and springing down the final flight into the hallway, now filled with smoke billowing out from the kitchen. Coughing, she veered sideways as she ran, heading for the front door. She heard the shrill beeping of the fire alarm and the sound of smashing, as Jo bashed into the photos coming down the stairs.

Luckily, the door was unlocked – thank God for the relative safety of the countryside – and she ran out on to the courtyard. Dawn had come and there was a soft grey light in the sky, the cawing of crows in the trees.

'Oh no,' she said, as she looked back and saw Jo come out of the doorway, running with terrifying speed, the scissors still clutched in his hand. He let out a strange yowl.

Her head was killing her, but the one thing Alice knew she could do was run.

She fled across the garden and into the trees, followed closely by the possessed howling man.

The woods were still gloomy, the dawn only just starting to penetrate the canopy with grainy light.

Alice swerved this way and that, leaping through the lighter patches of bramble and undergrowth that she had started to get a feel for over the last few days, wending her way up towards higher ground. She had no plan, her only thought was to outrun him. How old was he? Between forty-five and fifty, she guessed. He was clearly fit for his age, probably why he'd chosen a career in sport. But she had the edge on him, and could hear him increasingly – albeit marginally – losing ground on her. She just had to keep her head.

She passed through the even darker area of rhododendrons and laurels, her naked feet squidging in the black soil.

'I'm going to get you, Alice!' she heard him bellow, maybe ten or fifteen metres behind now.

'Not if I can help it,' she muttered.

Soon she was running alongside the foundation of the old smallpox hospital, heading ever upwards, towards the brightness breaking through the taller, more feathery pines. She risked a glance round, saw that Jo – Eloise – was at least ten metres behind, just reaching the edge of the demolished wall.

And then her right foot landed square on a stone she hadn't seen and she yelped in pain.

'Shit!'

She jerked her knee up, slowing rapidly to reduce the agony in the arch of her foot. She heard a gleeful cackle from behind her.

She had to keep going! She sprinted again, crying out with the pain of it. Was it broken, bleeding? No time to think, he was gaining on her again. It just… hurt so much…

A short way above her the light grew sharper, pinker, a sign that she was nearing the edge of the trees, the place where the cliff fell away to the sea. What could she do? She gasped with every step she took, slowing, slowing…

Now she could hear him panting behind her, evidently tired too. They had been running for what felt like ages, as fast as they could. What was she going to do? Her face made a rictus of pain each time her injured foot struck the ground.

She reached the cliff edge path, saw the soft silver sea just beyond the thin line of trees. The sky was mauve, pink, peach, grey. She looked left and right, desperate to find something, a stone, a stick, with which to defend herself. There was nothing.

Gasping for breath, grimacing in agony, she turned to face her crazed pursuer.

86.

He had stopped too, panting, with his hands on his knees.

Looking up at her.

'Well, Alice,' he said. 'Looks like we're there now.'

As he straightened his back, she saw that he was still clutching the scissors. The dressmaker's shears.

'What is so wrong… about crossing over?' she said, gasping for breath.

'Do you like the idea of going somewhere you don't know?' said the Welshman, his Valleys accent taking on a strange lilt as Eloise spoke through him. 'Forever? What if it's hellish? Or, even worse, boring?'

She shook her head slowly. Perhaps she should yell at him, try to shock the ghost out of him like the quadbiker?

'When all you want to do is have fun here?' he continued.

'Fun? You call what you do fu…'

She screamed as the man – *Eloise* – ran at her, the scissors high. As he lunged, she ducked aside, escaping the downward blow but colliding heavily with him. The momentum of his strike spun her round, off balance, and she thrust him blindly away, before falling backwards into the dirt.

Jo overshot the path and stumbled on the slippery, needle-strewn bank. Realising what was coming, his arm came out for one of the trees, a straggly young sycamore.

His outstretched fingers touched the thin trunk as he lurched forwards over the edge.

He glanced around sharply and Alice saw a desperate, cursing look in his eyes as he ran into the air.

Not the look of a middle-aged man, but of someone else entirely.

And then he – *she* – was gone.

87

'Alice! Alice – stop!'

She felt a hand on her shoulder, glanced round at Aitor, shook herself loose as she continued to pace along the cliff edge. Clutching a tree trunk, she leaned out to peer down at the rocks and sea below.

'He's down there, I have to watch, he's going to come up,' she said.

'Alice… who? Who's down there?'

'Jo – Eloise – she possessed him. They fell, they're down there…'

'Alice, stop, stop, you're hysterical.'

She felt him pull her back from where she hung heavily out over the drop. She stumbled backwards a little with him, and then they had both fallen and were sitting side by side on the path.

'What happened Alice?' said Aitor, holding her face to look at him.

'He – she – came at me with the scissors.'

'What did you do?'

'I dodged them.'

'Good.'

'But then we collided – and I pushed him away – and he couldn't stop.' Tears streamed from her eyes.

Aitor looked at her and then pulled her face against his shoulder, holding her tight.

'He went over the edge?' he said quietly.

Her face was soaking now, she wanted to sob so hard that she could scarcely breathe.

After a moment he said: 'Listen, you have to tell me what happened. Quickly.'

'The house!' she exclaimed suddenly. 'Susannah – and Jacob…'

'We put the fire out with the extinguishers,' he said. 'Susannah and Jacob are safe, the fire brigade is coming. Susannah told me about Jo trying to attack her and the appearance of the man in the suit.'

'Aitor – she possessed me! That witch girl took over my body!'

'What?'

'Eloise – the girl from Farthingbridge – when I woke up she had… *invaded* me. I was trapped inside a part of my mind. It was horrible. I could see what she was doing, I could see inside *her*, but I couldn't stop her.'

'She made you set fire to the house?'

'Yes! And I tried – she tried – to kill Susannah! But Dominic saved her – by coming at me. I fell over and hit my head and blacked out. When I came to, Eloise had left me and taken over Jo. He tried to stab Susannah but I distracted him and ran. He chased me here…'

'He wanted you more than her?' said Aitor.

'Yes. She was haunting me because she wanted to kill me. When we encountered each other she'd seen what I did to the ghosts at Bramley and was terrified I would somehow force her out of this world, into the next. She wanted to stay around. Aitor – she was so corrupted – she loved darkness.'

'And now she's gone,' said Aitor.

'How can you be sure?'

'I can't, but I'm guessing that she had no time to leave him. She was… unprepared. And you were aware of her, conscious of how she worked – so she couldn't get back into you.'

Alice shook her head.

'Ghosts who possess people who die, die themselves,' he said.

'How do you know?'

'I don't for sure.'

'Sounds like the end of *The* bloody *Exorcist*,' said Alice.

'Yes,' said Aitor. 'But look, Alice, we have to sort out our story, fast. And the first thing is, you must realise it wasn't you who killed Jo.'

Her face crumpled again. 'I shouldn't have pushed him away. I could have saved him.'

'No. You couldn't. He was possessed. It was either you or him – her, Eloise, in reality – and you acted instinctively to save yourself. There was nothing else you could have done. Nothing.'

'So what? Are you saying I have to lie?'

'You can only tell part of the truth. Because no one would ever believe the whole of it.'

She closed her eyes, feeling the faintest breeze on her face.

'Just tell me what to do,' she whispered, wishing for a moment she could just step away like Jo, and vanish into the soft sea below.

88.

There were two fire engines, two police cars and an ambulance all parked in the drive when they got back to Peacehaven.

Alice spotted Susannah in the back of the ambulance, looking haggard and talking to two paramedics. A policeman stood discreetly nearby. Another policeman and a policewoman were playing with Jacob, pushing him around on the toy tractor. Two firemen were emerging from the front of the house.

'You can do this,' said Aitor under his breath, as the two of them approached the police officers to tell them to call the coastguard.

89.

When the policeman and woman interviewed her, Alice told them how she had woken to shouts from downstairs and gone down to find Jo in Susannah's room, advancing on her with a pair of scissors. She told them how she'd tried to stop him but he'd knocked her down. She shouted at him from the ground and he turned on her, a strange, glazed expression on his face. When he began to chase her instead, she had run as fast as she could out of the house and into the woods, all the time pursued by him. She told them how he had caught up with her when she hurt her foot. How she had narrowly avoided his charge at her when she was standing at the edge of the cliff. How he had run on, and fallen.

'Do you have any idea why he would have tried to attack you or Mrs Parry?' asked the policewoman.

Alice shook her head. 'All I can say is that he was a lovely man. I'd spoken to him a few times before, he had always been a real gentleman. I believe – from the look in his eyes that night – that he was not himself.'

'What do you mean?' said the policeman.

'He looked like he was completely out of it,' said Alice. She felt physically sick as she held the young man's gaze. 'Like he was sleep walking. I think he did it all in his sleep, or in some kind of trance. In fact, I'm sure of it. I can't see the man I met having any reason to do any of those things.'

90.

A couple of hours later all their statements had been taken and the police had gone. Just before they left, Alice had had a short argument with the paramedics who wanted to take her in because of the cut and bruising on her foot, but she had refused and in the end they had just cleaned and bandaged it for her. Alice and Susannah were now sitting on the terrace at the back of the house, whilst Aitor headed inside to dismantle his equipment.

As the Basque man disappeared into the kitchen, Alice turned to Susannah and said:

'You knew all along, didn't you?'

'What?'

'Who he was – the ghost haunting your guests. It was Dominic, your old business partner. He was here to get revenge on you for all that you did to him. For how you manipulated him, how you made him fall for you and then sign away most of the business to you. You didn't care about him – or his family. You just cared about yourself. About getting enough money to start your next thing.' She looked across at Jacob, stacking odd-shaped stones on the edge of the terrace steps.

Susannah gazed at her, her green eyes impassive.

'I bet you even saw him didn't you?' said Alice. 'You just didn't tell me because… Oh, I don't know. I suppose you hoped I'd magic up some solution to get rid of him, without ever finding out who he really was.' She remembered the expression on Susannah's face at Oxwich when Alice described how she'd helped Mary cross over by understanding what was holding her back. The concern.

Susannah tugged at a few strands of her hair. 'He's been following me for years,' she said quietly. 'The dirty little creep.'

Alice stared at her dumbfounded. After a moment she said: 'But you didn't count on Aitor.'

'Don't lecture me, Alice.'

'What? Don't lecture you? You –' Alice wanted to swear, but she remembered the little boy playing on the step. She hissed with disbelief, wondering how many other people Susannah had screwed over in her life. 'You know the irony?' she continued. 'He still loved you. Maybe – who knows how this life and death thing works – maybe still *loves* you!'

'Don't freak me out,' said Susannah.

'He saved you,' said Alice quietly.

'What do you mean?'

Alice knew she couldn't tell her the full story – of how Dominic had startled her when she was possessed and about to kill Susannah – without incriminating herself.

'When Jo was coming at you, he was possessed. By an evil spirit. We can never prove it, so you'll just have to take my word for it. Dominic came back to try and save you. I saw him. I suspect you saw him too. But he didn't manage it. So I had to save you instead.'

Susannah screwed up her face. 'I've had enough of all this paranormal crap,' she said. Then as they sat there, staring at the woods, she said: 'Do you think he'll be back?'

'I don't know,' said Alice. 'But if it wasn't for your lovely little boy – and your husband – I have to say, I wouldn't give a damn if he was.'

Susannah got out her cigarettes, drew one out of the pack, and lit it with a plastic lighter. She blew smoke out across the table. 'He was a pathetic excuse for a man,' she said. 'Always moaning about his wife and child, never making any decisions. The company would have been nothing without me. Zilch.'

Alice studied her for a moment. 'You haven't changed one bit, have you?' she said.

Susannah gave her a thin-lipped smile, as Aitor appeared from around the side of the house.

91.

Whilst Aitor was loading his car, Alice went up to the Reading room to pack her things.

As soon as she was alone in the room an image of Jo stumbling past her flashed in her mind. She felt a heat on her palm, as if the weave of his cotton T-shirt was burning there.

She pushed him…

'Stupid, so stupid,' she muttered to herself, shoving her crumpled clothes, jeans, underwear, tops, her washbag and hairbrush, into her duffle bag.

She froze, as a hand appeared on top of hers. It was a man's hand, with slender fingers, carefully pared nails. She could see the fine half-moons, the absence of cuticle.

She drew in a breath, and looked up into the grotesque face of the hanged man. Dominic Turner.

'What are you doing?' she said. She turned away sharply, then forced herself to look back into those swollen, blood-soaked eyes. Fighting away panic.

The ghost was wincing, gritting his teeth, then his ruddy face drooped and a sorrowful, pleading look, like a mournful dog, appeared in his eyes.

'I – I don't know what I can do for you,' she stammered.

He continued to stand there, by the bed, in the soft sunlight. It was as if he was hovering, only partially held by the pull of gravity. Alice half expected him to rise away from the floor.

'Look,' she said. 'You have to leave here. I know what she did to you. It was unforgivable. But – well, she's just like that. She's one of those people who you kind of fall in love with – but they let you down. They just use you. I guess she's a kind of sociopath, or narcissist, or something.'

He was shaking his head slowly, his eyes imploring.

'But you can't make her family suffer. Her son. Her husband. I suspect they're going to suffer enough just… just because of who she is.' She thought about Gareth, wondered how much his near-breakdown was caused by the ghost and finances, and how much by a wife whose true character he must surely know by now.

'But they had nothing to do with all this,' she continued. 'And you were at fault too. Look what you did to your own family. You mustn't ruin any more lives.'

She thought he would be angry with this, but instead his eyes swelled and his mouth, with the revolting green, almost purple tongue, opened even wider in horror. As he gave the agonising yawn she could see his molars, white, clean, at the back of his mouth. He was scared, disgusted, hateful – hateful of… of what? Himself? His actions?

'Go now,' said Alice quietly. 'You've suffered more than enough.'

With that she looked down and stuffed her towel, still damp, and her swimming gear into her bag. When she looked up again, the room was empty.

As she had expected.

92.

'Is Gareth still coming back today?'

'Yes, I'm going to go and collect him now.'

The sunlight seemed to brighten as Alice looked up at her former friend, standing in the doorway of Peacehaven. She felt her throat catch, a sting around the corners of her eyes. Susannah, with her sea-green irises and neat blonde hair was beautiful, aloof, callous and… infuriating. Alice could weep – or scream – but instead she said:

'Goodbye Susannah.'

'Goodbye Alice.'

Jacob came out from behind his mother's legs and stumbled forward a couple of steps. Alice stroked his hair, then turned around and climbed into the passenger seat of Aitor's car.

Alice and Susannah watched each other for a few moments, as Aitor revved a little too harshly, then drove her away.

93

They didn't get far before Aitor had to pull up off the road in a gateway and put his arm around her.

'I just can't seem to stop,' she said, rubbing the tears away with her sleeve. 'Sorry.'

'It's no problem, darling,' said the Basque. 'Let it out.'

She was crying hard, trying to hold her breath to contain it. 'Everything would have been OK if I'd gone with my initial feeling,' she said.

'What do you mean?'

'To ignore it.'

'Ignore what?'

'Her email. Susannah's email to me. I should just have let it go, but instead I brought *her* – Eloise – here. And now… now Jo's dead.'

Aitor looked across the top of her head, out at the open countryside, the flat grassy fields with luscious trees and hedges. 'You could never have known that,' he said, finally. 'And who knows, there may be more good that comes from it. Eloise is gone. Dominic is almost certainly gone. There are good things,' he repeated. 'And the bad could not have been foreseen.'

Alice bit her lip, listening to him, staring at the dashboard.

Epilogue

Three Weeks Later

The day of Jo's funeral began with strong, cold rain, but by the time they carried his coffin out into the little hilltop cemetery the sun was streaming through the pines, gleaming on the damp headstones.

Alice, dressed in a short grey cotton dress, stood there at the graveside as the young priest went through the *dust to dust* ritual. He was trying to be loud, grave, but his voice was not as deep as he would have liked and every so often his pitch went high. There were only four people there, Jo's uncle, a plumber from Hay, an elderly female neighbour with a chihuahua in her arms, and two colleagues from the climbing centre. They had all chatted politely before the ceremony began, but it had become clear to Alice that Jo had no close family or friends. That might explain why he was holidaying alone. She struggled not to give in to a growing sense of desolation.

This body in a box, who had lived in the good world.

The good world that Alice continued to gaze around at, the pine-needle scent she breathed in, the sunshine she felt heating her skin.

'…in sure and certain hope of the resurrection to eternal life,' the priest continued.

She had thought all ghosts were sad, tethered to the world by injustice. But now she knew: ghosts could be bad as well as good. They could chew you up and spit you out and leave you feeling as empty as the starless sky. And ghosts could just be ordinary, their motives as selfish and mixed up as the living.

Alice thought about Femi, out of her coma, but signed off on long-term sick leave. And of Mike, with his increasing drinking and long periods of absence from work. What demons were they dealing with?

The same demons that she was now battling nightly. The demons of guilt. For her, the terrible, soul-crushing guilt of having played a part in a man's death. For having survived, when Jo had died. She would tell them both the truth of what had happened, of their possession by the girl in the ivory dress, if she could. But she would have to deal with it herself first.

'…who will transform our frail bodies, that they may be conformed to his glorious body…'

And betrayal. That also kept her awake at night. As the priest finished the committal and the small crowd turned back towards the chapel, Alice thought about betrayal. She thought of what had happened to her in Bramley. And she thought about Susannah. She remembered that old adage: fool me once, shame on you. Fool me twice, shame on me.

Never again.

She shielded her eyes from the sun and looked out across the valley. And saw the broad River Cynon meandering away, down, always down, through trees and villages and fields, down on its glistening journey towards the sea.

Thank you for reading my book, I hope you enjoyed it!

If you did I would really appreciate it if you could post a rating or write a short review on Amazon or Goodreads. Your ratings make a huge difference to authors, helping the books you enjoy reach more people.

The Ghosts *of* Alice

The Ghosts of Alice is a new set of standalone ghost stories featuring Alice Deaton, a young woman with a mysterious connection to the dead.

The Boy *in the* Burgundy Hood

** THE #1 INTERNATIONAL BESTSELLER **

Will it be her dream job – or a waking nightmare?

Alice can't believe her luck when she lands a new post at a medieval English manor. Mired in debt, the elderly owners have transferred their beloved Bramley to a heritage trust. Alice must prepare it for opening to the public, with the former owners relegated to a private wing.

But when the ghosts start appearing - the woman with the wounded hand and the boy in the burgundy hood - Alice realises why her predecessor might have left the isolated house so soon.

As she peels back the layers of the mystery, the secrets Alice uncovers haunting Bramley's heart will be dark - darker than she could ever have imagined…

Alice *and the* Devil

'Yes, I can see ghosts,' she said.
'That's why she told me to come here. Because you can help us.
You can help grandad and me. You can help us defeat him.'
'Him?'
'Yes, him. The Devil.'

A boy crosses the moors in a storm to plead for Alice's help, claiming to be sent by a ghost.

Is the boy's grandfather really being terrorised by the Devil himself? Alice can't quite believe it – but then she's experienced things she'd never imagined could come true. But even with her paranormal experiences, little does she expect the horror she is about to face at the lonely rectory overlooking the moors…

Standalone Supernatural Thrillers

Black Beacon: *A Christmas Ghost Story*

1976. The South Downs.
The Christmas it snowed.
The Christmas that evil returned…

Struggling with money, Theo and Nat are doing their best to make Christmas special. It's been a hard time of year for them, ever since they lost their beloved daughter.

But this year, their troubles are just beginning. They are about to be visited by a terrifying ghost from Christmas past, a spirit that will bring back not just the horror of the war that divided them but also a deep, hidden betrayal from their early life together…

The Man *in the* Woods

Who is the Man in the Woods?

The woods are deep and dark and cold and empty…
… except for a solitary boy, out riding his bike…
… and a lone wanderer…
What will happen when their paths cross?

Whatever it is, things will never be the same again.

About the Author

Steve Griffin is the author of fourteen books, known for his supernatural thrillers full of 'twists and turns' including the bestselling Ghosts of Alice series and The Man in the Woods. His latest book is Black Beacon, a chilling Christmas ghost story set on the snow-swept South Downs.

He has also written a fast-paced adventure mystery series for young adults, The Secret of the Tirthas. A Guardian review of the first book, The City of Light, calls it 'entertaining and exciting'.

Steve loves exploring the Surrey Hills, where he lives with his wife and two sons. He also enjoys a good indie gig and is a lifelong fan of horror movies.

To keep updated on his writing, hit the follow button on Amazon or sign up to his newsletter by emailing stevegriffin.author@outlook.com. You can also check out his website at steve-griffin.com, or follow him on Instagram and Facebook (@stevegriffin.author).

Printed in Great Britain
by Amazon